YOU'RE THE MAIN CHARACTER. YOU MAKE THE CHOICES.
CAN YOU SURVIVE?

GREEK MYTHOLOGY'S
TWELVE LABORS OF
HERCULES

Minneapolis, Minnesota

Dedication

To my mom, who instilled in me a love of stories
and of Greek mythology.

Edited by Dana Kuznar
Cover art by David Hemenway
Cover logo by Shane Nitzsche

10 9 8 7 6 5 4 3 2 1

Library of Congress Control Number: 2013934773

Published by Lake 7 Creative, LLC
Minneapolis, MN 55412
www.lake7creative.com

ISBN: 978-0-9883662-9-9

Dear Reader,

When I was in fourth grade, I found a book in my school library that I couldn't put down. On its cover was a man who looked stronger than any superhero in my favorite comic books. He wore a lion's head on his own. He carried a giant wooden club. And he was fighting a menacing, serpent-like creature. That man was Hercules, and because of that book, I became a lifelong fan of Greek mythology.

Hercules is one of the best known characters from Greek mythology. He is the star of movies, television shows, books, and comics. This is an introduction to one of the world's first superheroes. I urge you to search out more about Hercules and the ancient Greek gods. Their stories are wildly entertaining.

I'm pleased to have been able to adapt a Choose Your Path book based on Hercules and his twelve labors. I hope you enjoy my retelling. I'll warn you, though. You best be prepared to fight serpents and giants and vicious, three-headed dogs. Happy reading!

—Brandon Terrell

How to Use This Book

As you read *Greek Mythology's Twelve Labors of Hercules*, you will sometimes be asked to jump to a distant page. Please follow these instructions. Sometimes you will be asked to choose between two or more options. Decide which you feel is best, and go to the corresponding page. (But be careful; some options will lead to disaster.) And finally, if a page offers no instructions or choices, simply go to the next page.

Enjoy the story, and good luck!

Table of Contents

Prologue:
Tyler Hammond

"Oh, no, I'm going to be late for class!"

You hurry through the crowded halls of your school. Around you, classmates gather books from their lockers and dash to their first morning classes. You are on your way to Ancient History. There's a big test today, and you've been studying hard for it.

As you race for class, you glance down at the textbook in your hands. You are hoping to study a bit more before you reach Mr. Jamieson's room. In fact, you are so engrossed in your book that you don't see Tyler Hammond until you've run right into him.

Tyler is a big kid, known around the school as a bully. He turns to face you, and you notice a giant red stain down the front of his T-shirt. He's holding a plastic bottle of soda. Liquid drips from the bottle and down his hand.

Tyler wipes his chin and sneers. "Watch where you're going, man."

"Ty—Ty—Tyler," you stammer. "I'm so sorry." Your heart thunders in your chest. Bravery is not one of your stronger traits.

"You better be," he says. He leans in close and adds, "I'd watch your back after school if I were you."

He walks past you, bumping you hard with his shoulder. You drop the textbook and quickly scoop it up just as the bell rings. Now you'll be late for sure.

All day, you can't help but think of Tyler. He's been known to pick fights, but you never thought you'd be on the other end of his fist. You're so distracted that you bomb your Ancient History test. Your friends try their best to cheer you up, but it doesn't work.

Finally, the last bell rings. Students fill the halls. Many head off to sports or band practice. Others stay at their lockers for a bit, chatting with friends.

You shove your books into your backpack and walk toward the main entrance, where the school buses are lined up. Maybe he's forgotten. Maybe Tyler has other plans and won't be looking for you.

Your hopes are dashed when you exit the school and see the bully standing right beside your bus. He is searching for you.

Turning, you burst back into the school and run down the halls, not caring where you go. You duck into the library and weave your way through its rows of shelves until you are hidden in a corner. There, you sit on the floor, draw up your knees, and wrap your arms around them.

Minutes pass. Your breathing finally slows, and your hands stop shaking.

And then you hear it. Sounds, quiet at first but gradually growing in volume. The roar of a lion. The clash of swords. The snarling of an angry dog.

As weird as it seems, the noises are coming from the shelf beside you. You search the books. They are old, dusty versions of classic stories: *The Merry Adventures of Robin Hood, 20,000 Leagues Under the Sea, Treasure*

Island, and more. You can't recall having seen any of these books here before.

The source of the sounds is a large book with green binding. In gold letters on the spine is the title: *Greek Mythology: The Twelve Labors of Hercules*. Will you take the book from the shelf and open it? Or will you ignore the strange noises? What will you choose to do?

To pick up the book, go to page 34.

To leave the book alone, go to page 82.

With your decision made, you tell Pholus, "I must be off to begin my hunt."

"Very well," he replies. "Let us stock you with fresh food. You will need your energy while climbing that cold rock."

Brom and another centaur gather extra food and water and add them to your things. You are also given extra furs with which to bundle yourself.

Pholus leads you to the mouth of the cave. In the distance, you see the snow-capped Mount Erymanthus. Pholus points to a formation of broken rocks and says, "You will find the boar there. Good luck, Hercules."

You shake the centaur's hand, then hurry down the winding dirt path once more.

You set up camp at the base of Mount Erymanthus. It is not terribly cold there, and with the extra skins and furs, you stay very warm.

The following morning, you begin to climb Mount Erymanthus. At times, the way is steep, and you must stop frequently to rest. The cold is bitter, but your extra food and drink fuel your energy. You will need your strength when you come face to face with the boar.

At last, you reach the area Pholus pointed toward. There, you wait.

Sure enough, the boar appears. It is a large creature with gnarled, bristling hair, a flat snout, and thick tusks. It looks unstoppable as it barrels toward you to attack. You quickly climb up the mountain.

You scramble over large boulders and through small clusters of trees. The boar is at your back, following each step you make. The terrain is rocky, though, and the boar can't gain enough footing to catch you.

Hour after hour, you wind your way up and down the mountain. The bloodthirsty boar never gives up the chase. At times, you even lead the beast through snow that is nearly up to your waist.

When you lose sight of the creature, you stop to scan your surroundings. It is nowhere around. Curious, you retrace your steps down the mountainside.

You find the beast in a snow bank. Its breathing puffs in clouds from its snout. The animal is so tired that it has fallen asleep.

You drag the sleeping boar down the mountainside and back to Mycenae.

When King Eurystheus sees you enter his room with the ghastly-looking pig, he leaps from his throne to hide.

"I told you to leave your prize at the city gate," the frightened king whimpers.

"You didn't feel that way about the golden deer," you say, a smile parting your lips.

"Yes, well, this creature smells of death!"

You laugh. "Say my labor is complete, and I will send the boar on its way."

"Yes, of course! Now be rid of it!"

You lead the Erymanthian Boar from the city in the same fashion as you did the golden deer. It does not leap and bound gracefully away, though. The squat, ugly beast barrels forward, crashing through trees and shrubs, leaving in its wake a path of snapped branches and trampled leaves.

Thus ends your fourth labor.

6

Birds of a Different Feather

Eurystheus next tries to humiliate you as payback for bringing the stinking boar to his feet. For the fifth labor, he sends you to Elis, to clean the stables of King Augeas—and you must finish in just one day.

King Augeas owns over one thousand cattle. When you reach his farmstead, you see three buildings made of wood. Each has a thin roof supported by nothing but thick posts made from tree trunks. Enormous piles of animal waste and filth spill from all three stables.

Augeas leads you to the foul stables. Swarms of flies buzz about. "The cattle are divinely healthy," he says, meaning they are magical and live very long lives. "The stables have not been cleaned in thirty years."

You notice a large river coursing past the farmstead. A plan forms in your mind. "I will have them clean," you boldly proclaim.

The king laughs and claps you on the shoulder. "Then let me get you a shovel."

"I will not need one." You cross between two of the ripe-smelling stables and to a thick rock wall. The wall separates the river from the king's land. You drive your shoulder into the stone, jarring some of the boulders loose. Thin trails of water trickle through the new gaps.

"What are you doing?" King Augeas exclaims.

"Cleaning your stables," you answer. "You may wish to move."

You push against the weakened barrier again. You can feel the river's powerful current about to break through. You hurry away and find a spot high on a hill. Then you watch as the rock wall gives way. The river crashes through with a mighty roar. The twisting, foaming water washes away the filth.

Hours later, the river's flow has waned, leaving the stable grounds clean. Every bit of manure has been washed away. You carefully rebuild the stone wall with heavy boulders, but King Augeas is not pleased with your methods. When you find him, he is standing ankle-deep in a puddle of water.

"It will take days for my stables to dry!"

"Yes, but they are clean, are they not?"

You bow to the king, then hurry back along the path to Mycenae.

"What is that foul stench?" King Eurystheus asks as you enter his chamber. He claps one hand over his mouth and nose.

"Apologies, cousin," you say. "That smell is me."

"Clean yourself. Then make your way to Arcadia. You'll find a forest near the town of Stymphalus. A lake has become the nesting grounds for a flock of birds that are destroying the land. Be rid of them."

"Aren't these birds the pets of Ares, god of war? The ones with deadly feathers used to kill their prey?"

"And what if they are?" the king answers. "You are still mine to command, Hercules, and you'll do as you're told. Now, be gone!"

"As you wish."

You take a day to rest and to scrub away the stench. Then you prepare for your next labor. Your wooden bow and quiver of arrows are ideal to use against the birds. You drape the lion's pelt over your shoulders and place its head atop your own. You carry a shield in one hand but leave your sword and club behind.

As you near the small town of Stymphalus, you see the effects of the birds on the land. The deadly birds have stripped trees to the bark, leaving them as skeletal frames that sway eerily in the breeze. The grassland you walk across is brown and crisp. It crunches underfoot. The farms you pass are ghostly, abandoned.

You spy one of the birds you seek. It is perched high atop a slanting wooden barn. The bird is larger than an eagle, with black, metallic wings, a red belly, and claws and beaks made of bronze.

You watch as the bird lifts into the air. Its wings are almost bat-like, thin and long. It glides high into the gray, cloudy afternoon sky.

A wild mutt with brown fur emerges from a farmhouse and lopes across the grassland. The bird sees it and dives. As the bird nears the mutt, one of its feathers splits from its wing and slices through the air. It strikes the mutt on its back, and the small animal goes down.

The bird swoops and grasps the lifeless mutt in its bronze claws. It lifts into the air, winging away from you, across a field of high reeds and grasses.

The bird is surely heading to its nesting grounds to share its meal with the flock. If you climb a tree, you will be able to watch the bird and get a sense of where it's going. You'll lose the bird eventually, but you will know which way to travel. Or you can follow it now. If you keep up with it, you'll find the flock at once. But if you can't keep up, you'll have nothing to show for it. What will you choose to do?

To climb the tree, go to page 38.

To follow the bird, go to page 57.

You dare not turn your back on the Hydra, even in its weakened condition. You raise your sword above your head and slash downward.

The Hydra exhibits a sudden alertness and safely recoils from your attack. Your sword slices nothing but air—and when it strikes the stony ground, the metal blade shatters in two.

A shiver of pain explodes through both arms. At the same moment, Iolaus cries out in pain behind you.

You turn to find his leg caught in the razor-sharp claw of the ancient crab.

"Hercules! Help me!"

The crab scuttles back toward the swamp, dragging Iolaus with it. You throw the broken hilt of your sword at the crab, but the sword bounces harmlessly off its shell. Before you can reach them, the crab and Iolaus disappear beneath the murky water of the swamp.

You race to the edge of the swamp, reach in with both hands, and try to find your young companion. You have no luck. He is gone.

Regret fills your heart. Even if you complete this task, you will never forget how you failed Iolaus.

Weaponless, you turn toward the Hydra. A large head strikes, its teeth sinking into your arm.

Burning pain sizzles, and then you lose all feeling. The numbness spreads, and you find that you can no longer move.

As the Hydra prepares to attack again, you realize that this is the end. You close your eyes and await the Hydra's final strike.

Go to page 83.

Iolaus is young and untested in battle. This journey will be far too dangerous. Your decision is an easy one.

"My answer is still no," you tell the boy. "Defeating the Hydra is my labor. I will face it alone."

Iolaus's shoulders slump. "Very well," he moans.

The road to Lernea is long and treacherous. On your way, you imagine the Hydra with its many heads, each with dangerous venom. One bite will paralyze a man in seconds. And the Hydra is immortal. It cannot be killed. You wonder how you will defeat such a creature.

At last, you come upon the marshes of Lernea. You walk among the high weeds and tall trees. A mist rises from the swamps. The stench is awful, so you take a bit of cloth and tie it tightly across your nose and mouth. Just in case the Hydra's breath truly is poisonous, this may protect you.

As you continue on your way, the sun sets. You have seen no sign of the Hydra, but it grows too dark to search any longer. You must rest for the night.

You huddle against a rock, rest your sword across your chest, and close your eyes.

Crack!

Your eyes snap open. Something stirs in the trees to your right. A shadow darts forward, and you don't have time to react. A large head strikes, its teeth sinking into your arm.

Burning pain sizzles, and you lose all feeling in your limb. You grab your sword with your good arm, and you blindly hack at the creature's neck.

The Hydra screeches in anger and pain, but then its head falls to the dirt in silence. You have defeated this midnight attacker.

Or have you?

The neck squirms back and forth. You watch as a pulsing mass of muscle emerges from the wound. The mass splits, grows, and shapes itself into two new heads!

The numbness spreads through your body, and you find that you can no longer move.

As the Hydra prepares to attack again, you realize that this is the end. You close your eyes and await the Hydra's final strike.

Go to page 83.

The oracle has spoken truth for centuries. And even if Hera is directing her words, the gods will surely make good on her promise.

And so, you bend a knee and bow your head. "As you wish," you say. "Thank you, great Pythia."

As you raise your head, though, you find that the oracle is no longer present. Wordlessly, you travel back through the mountain and again into daylight.

2
The Labors Begin

The walled city of Mycenae rests upon a hill and is surrounded by farmland. As you approach, you see the king's palace looming above its kingdom. Armored guards with swords meet you at the gates.

"I am here to see the king," you tell them. "I am his cousin, Hercules."

Recognition lights in their eyes at the mention of your name. Immediately, the guards usher you to the palace and into King Eurystheus's throne room.

The king is a thin man with beady eyes and sunken features. Sitting on his marble throne, he appears like a bird in a nest. Around him are treasures and weapons. He does not stand to greet you.

"Cousin," King Eurystheus says. The single word drips with disgust.

You take a knee. "My lord."

"To what do I owe this visit?"

"I seek immortality so that I may take my place among the gods on Mount Olympus. To achieve this, the oracle at Delphi has sent me to you, that you may find purpose for my strength."

"Is that so?" The king barks a high, sharp laugh. It echoes through the chamber. "Then I shall find for you twelve labors, twelve amazing tasks. And I know just where you shall begin."

The king crosses the palace chamber to you. He is much shorter than you, yet his presence fills the room. He smiles, his lips stretching thin across his pale face.

"Near the village of Nemea, there is a lion roaming the countryside. This savage animal has been stealing livestock in the night and has begun to hunt townsfolk as well. Bring me the skin of this creature."

A lion? Is that all? The task seems simple. All you need is a sword at your side. With one swing, the deed will be done.

"I understand, my lord. I will leave at once."

You are about to exit when Eurystheus stops you. "About this creature," he adds, "the lion is magical. Its skin cannot be cut by blade or spear."

"Nevertheless, I will bring its hide to you."

You arm yourself with a club carved from the finest olive tree and a sword from the palace. Then you begin the long trek southeast, to the village of Nemea.

When you arrive, you find it nearly deserted. Very few townsfolk dare to step from their homes, and those who do move quickly to their destinations.

As you track the lion, you see some of the damage it has done. One farm has a broken fence, and the earth is still stained by the blood of lost livestock. At another, you spy a man and wife staring at you from a window. Even from a distance, you notice the fear in their eyes.

At last, you find trampled grass and shrubs leading into a copse of trees. A trail. And it's fresh.

The trail winds into the deep shadows of a forest. You come upon a stone clearing at the base of a cliff—and a cave. Littered about its entrance are the bones of animals and humans alike.

At the cave entrance, you ready your weapon. "Foul creature," you cry, "come out and face me!"

For a long while, nothing happens. Then a low rumbling growl emits from the cave. Two yellow eyes stare out at you.

Suddenly, the lion pounces. It soars at you with lean muscles rippling beneath its hide. Its claws spread and its jaw gapes open, displaying teeth as sharp as razors.

You stand your ground, and as the lion reaches you, you swing the club with all your strength. The creature is knocked away.

Your blow should have ended the beast. Instead, the lion is merely stunned.

"The king spoke the truth," you mutter, drawing the sword from your belt. "Let us try something sharper, shall we?"

The lion rises. It shakes its head, faces you, and lets out a mighty roar. You charge, hefting the sword over your head. You swing downward at the creature.

The lion twists its body, swatting at your weapon with its enormous paw. Its blow connects, sending a shuddering pain down both your arms. The sword is swept from your grasp. It clatters across the stony ground. You are unarmed, and the lion crouches in anticipation of striking again.

To your left, just out of reach, is the sword. To your right is the entrance to the creature's lair. Should you reach for your weapon? Or will you escape into the cave? What will you choose to do?

To grab your sword, go to page 46.

To hide within the cave, go to page 52.

You pluck a stone the size of your fist from a rock pile and step out from your hiding place. Holding the metal shield high above your head, you rap the stone loudly against it. The piercing sound echoes across the lake.

The birds take flight at once, turning the sky from gray to black. They swoop about, searching for the source of the noise. You draw your bow, notch an arrow, aim for the nearest bird, and take your shot.

The arrow hits its mark but only scratches the beast's metallic wing. The bird turns, swooping toward you. It releases one of its feathers. You raise your shield, and the poisonous feather bounces off with a soft clang.

More birds swarm around you. You fire arrow after arrow, trying hard to strike them down. You are able to kill a few of them, but it is not enough. And you are running out of arrows.

A rain of feathers cascades down on you. You are forced to drop your bow and hide beneath the lion pelt on your shoulders. You feel the feathers harmlessly bounce off the cloak.

A rattling noise, loud as thunder, echoes through the marsh. The birds caw angrily, but their attack ceases.

You glance from under the lion pelt and see a woman standing beside you. She looks powerful, with flowing robes and beautiful red hair. In her hands is a slender rattle made of bronze. She is Athena, goddess of courage and wisdom.

"Goddess, I thank you for your help," you say. You look up and see that the birds, startled by the noise, are keeping a fair distance.

She offers you the rattle. "This is a krotala, forged by Hephaestus, blacksmith to the gods. There is little sense in killing without cause," Athena explains. "With this, you will frighten away the birds."

You lift the rattle high into the air and shake it back and forth. The piercing sound it emits makes the birds recoil in fear.

You shout in triumph, and turn to thank Athena. The goddess is nowhere to be found.

With renewed strength, you climb the tallest pine tree in the nesting grounds. When you are high enough to touch the clouds, you brandish the rattle and give it a mighty shake. The nearest birds fly wildly, bumping into one another.

Sensing defeat, the remaining members of the flock caw at you. They turn as one and fly off. You watch until they are merely black dots in the sky. Then you safely descend from your perch.

You have done it. Ares's pets will no longer terrorize the land of Stymphalus.

Go to page 62.

If what you heard of the blood is true, one drop will kill you. That's far too risky. You gather your gear and place the Hydra's immortal head in a woolen sack.

Dawn breaks across the swamplands. Carrying the sack over your shoulder, you return along the same path, back toward your chariot.

At the edge of the swamp, you halt. Kneeling, you dig into the dirt with both hands and scoop out chunks of earth and stone. Then you place the sack containing the Hydra's immortal head into the hole and fill in the earth around it. Once it is buried, you heft several large boulders onto the site.

"Why have you buried your prize?" Iolaus asks.

"It is no prize," you say. "That head is immortal. But this way, the beast will remain dead."

"But Hercules," Iolaus says, "you will have no proof of your victory to show King Eurystheus."

"You fought at my side. Your word will be enough."

Together, you and Iolaus walk along the rutted path and into the daylight.

Go to page 48.

You may not get another opportunity like this. You notch an arrow into your bow, draw back the string, and let go. The deer leaps high, then falls to the ground beside the stream.

You actually hit it! You dash across the clearing and kneel beside the fallen animal. Your arrow has pierced its heart.

You grasp the creature's golden antlers and lift it from the ground. It is heavy, but you hoist the dead deer over your shoulders with ease.

"How dare you?" The voice comes from behind.

Suddenly, the forest is alive with activity. Trees sway back and forth, and the wind howls. You turn to find a beautiful woman standing near you. She is young, tall, and clothed in a green dress and hunting boots. Her brown hair is pulled back, held in place by a crown made of leaves. A golden bow is slung over one shoulder. She is the goddess of the hunt.

"Artemis," you gasp, as the deer falls from your shoulders, back to the earth.

"How dare you kill my prized animal?"

Your heart races. "I—I did not know that the deer belonged to you."

"A creature this beautiful? This unique? How could it not belong to a goddess?"

You have been so foolish! You think back to King Eurystheus's words. He never ordered you to kill the creature, only to fetch it.

"I'm truly sorry," you say.

"It is not enough," Artemis answers. "I do not care that you're Zeus's son. Your punishment will fit your crime. Hades, king of the Underworld, will be your judge now."

Artemis moves with such speed that you don't have time to react. She fires a golden arrow at you with amazing quickness. It slices through the air and strikes your chest.

You fall to the hard-packed earth, landing beside the golden deer. Your last thought is of Mount Olympus. And then there is eternal darkness.

Go to page 83.

Curiosity gets the better of you. You forget about Tyler Hammond and instead think about what might happen when you open the book.

You slide the book from its place on the shelf, and the sounds grow louder. The book is heavier than you expected, and it smells musty and old.

Suddenly, the book begins to shake. You do your best to hold onto it. The cover flies open on its own, and the lights in the library flicker and dim. You feel yourself being drawn into the book—as if invisible hands are reaching for you. The room spins. And then you see nothing but the book. You hear nothing but the lion, the sword fight, and the crack of thunder.

Everything goes black.

Go to the next page.

1
To Be Immortal

"Welcome, Hercules," says the woman seated before you. She is the most beautiful you've ever seen. Crimson robes flow about her. In one hand, she clutches a wreath. Her name is Pythia, and she is known throughout the land as the great Oracle of Delphi.

Pythia's temple is located deep within the slopes of Mount Parnassus in Greece. You have traveled far to speak with the oracle.

You are Hercules. Your mother is a mortal woman named Alcmene. Your father is Zeus, king of the gods. This means that you are a mortal with super-strength. You have been raised in the Greek village of Thebes in a time of gods, magic, and monsters.

Pythia speaks again. Her voice is thin, a whisper. "What answers do you seek?"

A pale mist escapes from cracks in the rock floor. The vapors twist about the oracle, encircling her body.

"I live in fear of my father's wife, the goddess Hera," you say. "As an infant, she sent serpents to my cradle in hope of killing me. She has tried to drive me mad. Soon, I am afraid she will succeed.

"And so," you continue, "I seek immortality. I am strong beyond measure, but I am also mortal. Were I to become immortal, I would never die. I could take my place beside Zeus atop Mount Olympus. I would not need to fear Hera any longer."

There is a hiss beneath your feet. You step back as a fresh plume of mist issues from the earth.

"Is this possible? Can I become immortal?"

Pythia does not answer. Instead, she gazes upon you. Her eyes are ink black, as dark as night.

A shape appears in the vapors behind the oracle. It is the outline of a figure, there and then gone. It looked like Hera! You wonder if it was really there at all or if the madness is creeping into your mind.

The oracle extends her arms to you. "Son of Zeus," she says. There is something different about the voice. It is almost as if someone is speaking through her. "Go to your cousin, King Eurystheus, who sits upon the throne in Mycenae. Do as he commands, and you will be granted the immortality you seek."

Eurystheus is a cruel, selfish king who ignores his kingdom's needs. Why would someone as wise as the oracle send you to serve such a vile lord? Could this be a trick? Is Hera speaking through the oracle? Yet, then again, if Pythia speaks the truth, do you dare pass up the chance to show the gods your courage and bravery, to prove yourself worthy once and for all? What will you choose to do?

To refuse the voice, go to page 44.

To trust the voice, go to page 22.

You will not rush foolishly after the winged beast. Instead, you will climb the tree and survey the land. You pull yourself up, limb by limb, branch by branch, until you are looking out over the grassy wasteland.

You spot a lake on the other side of the tall grasses. On the far side of the lake, the bird lands in a copse of pines. The flock emerges, swarming around the mutt. There are several dozen birds.

You scurry back down the dead tree and circle your way around the lake. There is an outcropping of rocks about one hundred yards from the nesting grounds. You hide behind it. Your plan is to draw the birds into the sky and fire your arrows at them.

If the arrows were dipped in blood, go to page 61.

If not, go to page 28.

As you weigh your decision, the screech of a bird echoes across the swampland. The nocturnal creature swoops above your head—so close that you feel the whisper of its wings against your face. You decide that it is better to face any foe by firelight than fall victim to an unseen attack.

"I see your point," you say. "You may light a fire."

Before long, a small fire crackles inside the circle of rocks. Its orange light shines across the clearing.

From the corner of your eye, you spy a shadow of movement. At first, you think it's just the light playing tricks on you. But then you see it again, a slithering black shape against the trees.

You draw your sword.

Iolaus leaps to his feet and scrambles backward. "What is it?" he squeaks.

"Our enemy."

The long shadow rises, and you see it clearly in the firelight. It is a thick, reptilian neck. At its end is the head of a serpent, unlike any you've seen before. Pointed snout. Black fangs. Yellow eyes.

The Hydra stands almost twenty feet tall. As it steps forward from the trees, many more of its heads emerge. There are nearly two-dozen of them. Each neck slithers in a different direction.

"Behind me," you say under your breath, and Iolaus cowers in your shadow.

The Hydra lashes out with one head, opening its black mouth wide and striking. You reach behind you, clutch Iolaus by the arm, and dart left. The beast's jaws snap shut in the space you just abandoned.

Without a second thought, you swing your sword and slice the serpent's head from its neck. It falls to the dirt and rolls out of sight.

The creature screeches in anger and pain. The neck squirms back and forth, but it does not bleed. Instead, a pulsing mass of muscle emerges from the wound. The mass splits, grows, and shapes itself into two new heads!

Behind you, Iolaus gasps. You sense his fear and can tell that he is about to flee.

You grasp his wrist and look into his eyes. "Calm yourself. I will make sure you're safe."

Iolaus nods and whispers, "I trust you."

The creature steps out from the trees. It has four, squat legs, like those of a great lizard. Beneath its feet, the edge of the clearing is nothing more than a pile of bones. They snap and crunch under the weight of the beast's every step.

Iolaus grabs a thick branch from the edge of the fire and wields it as a weapon. Its end burns red with flames, and the nearest Hydra head recoils away from it.

This gives you an idea.

"Iolaus, keep your torch ready," you command. "I will need your help."

Iolaus nods as the torch shakes in his hands. You ignore his fright and advance on the nearest head. The Hydra strikes, and as before, you dodge its jaws. Again you slice the head from its neck. This time, though, you grasp the wriggling neck and drag it to Iolaus.

"Seal the wound with fire," you shout. "Quickly!"

Squeezing his eyes shut, Iolaus places the flaming torch against the serpent's wound. It sizzles and smokes. The beast roars from this fresh pain, and the Hydra's neck tries to pull itself free, but you do not let it.

Finally, Iolaus draws back the torch. The neck is burned and blackened, and no new heads emerge.

"It—it worked," Iolaus says.

"Then we shall make quick work of this serpent," you say with a smile.

You swing your sword again and attack the creature with all of your might. One by one, you hack the heads off the Hydra and seal the neck with your companion's torch. When the flame sputters and begins to die out, Iolaus draws out a new log from the fire.

Soon, there are just two heads remaining, including the Hydra's immortal head. It is different from the others: larger, with great nostrils that flare with each breath.

The beast is wounded. Its movements are slow and labored. The immortal head slithers near, close enough that one mighty swipe will end the creature once and for all.

"Hercules, behind you!" Iolaus cries out.

You turn in time to see a new foe at the far side of the clearing. It is a giant crab with eight long legs. It scuttles toward you, opening and closing its sharp, curved claws.

"We must have angered Hera," you say to Iolaus. "She has sent a vicious creature to distract me from my labor."

The crab is heading directly for Iolaus. Will you have enough time to defeat the Hydra before the crab attacks your companion? Or should you turn your attention away from the Hydra and attack the crab? What will you choose to do?

To attack the Hydra, go to page 18.

To attack the crab, go to page 70.

There is no doubt that you saw Hera in the vapors. She must be whispering commands to the oracle—and you will not fall into her trap.

"I refuse," you say.

The oracle is taken aback. "No one has ever dared to refuse me," she says.

At her feet, a fresh plume of mist escapes the cracks in the temple's floor. The cloud encircles Pythia, making it hard to see anything. Then she is gone.

"Show yourself, Hera," you say, balling your hands into fists.

Stepping out of the mist in front of you is Zeus's wife, the jealous and unforgiving Hera. She is tall and beautiful, with wavy brown hair pulled back. Her face is grim, and there is an evil look in her eyes.

"You are not easy to trick," Hera says. "However, you should have listened to the oracle." A wide, malicious smile spreads across her face. She places her hands at her side, palms down. The mist grows more intense.

The ground begins to shake. Stones crack off the temple's walls and crash at your feet. One of the carved pillars crumbles and falls, shattering before you.

If you do not escape the temple now, it will be your tomb. Turning, twisting, you search for the entrance.

A chunk of rock strikes you in the shoulder. Pain flares through your arm and chest. You stumble this way and that.

You see the black doorway of the temple dimly in the mist, and you stagger toward it. You are only feet away when the entrance collapses. Rocks and debris rain down, sealing the temple off completely.

There is no way out now. You are buried alive.

Go to page 83.

You lunge for the sword. But as your fingers wrap around its hilt, the lion pounces. It is quicker than you thought. In extending your arm, you have exposed your midsection, and the lion finds this weakness.

Its powerful jaws clamp down upon your side. The pain is immediate. You hear your ribs snap and feel your life draining away.

Desperate, you swing the sword with one arm. The metal blade bounces off the lion harmlessly, and the beast bites down harder.

You try to breathe, but it's no use. There will be no immortality for you. You close your eyes and let the blackness of death wash over you.

Go to page 83.

If you coat your weapons with the blood, it may help you later on. You will not waste such an opportunity.

Iolaus brings your quiver of arrows, and you dip each arrowhead into the red pool. When this task is complete, you place the Hydra's immortal head in a woolen sack.

Dawn breaks across the swamplands. Carrying the sack over your shoulder, you return along the same path, back toward your chariot.

At the edge of the swamp, you halt. Kneeling, you dig into the dirt with both hands and scoop out chunks of earth and stone. Then you place the sack containing the Hydra's immortal head into the hole and fill in the earth around it. Once it is buried, you heft several large boulders onto the site.

"Why have you buried your prize?" Iolaus asks.

"It is no prize," you say. "That head is immortal. But this way, the beast will remain dead."

"Hercules," Iolaus says, "you will have no proof of your victory to show King Eurystheus."

"You fought at my side. Your word will be enough."

Together, you and Iolaus walk along the rutted path and into the daylight.

4

The Deer with the Golden Antlers

"You did what?"

King Eurystheus's words echo across the spacious throne room. He is seated in his marble throne. Beside him stands his herald, a bald man known as Copreus. You and young Iolaus bow before the king.

"Iolaus was a great help in defeating the Hydra," you say.

"He's just a boy, Hercules! How dare you put his life in danger?"

"He fought bravely and should be rewarded."

Iolaus's chest puffs out with pride at your claim.

"Your labor was to be done by you and you alone, Hercules." King Eurystheus stands and steps down from the throne. He waves a hand dismissively. "You may go, boy."

Iolaus rises. "As you wish, my lord." Your young companion nods to you, then takes his leave.

Eurystheus motions for you to stand, so you do.

"Cousin Hercules," the king says, "you have proven your strength against the lion and Hydra. So, for your next labor, you will go to Ceryneia. Alone. There, in the forest, you will fetch the golden hind for me."

The request confuses you. "A deer? Compared to the many-headed Hydra, this labor seems simple."

"The hind is mysterious. It has golden antlers and hooves of bronze. Few have ever seen the animal. This labor will require more than brute strength. Are you not up to the challenge?"

"I certainly am, my lord. I will track this deer and return to you, carrying the beast over my shoulder."

The king smiles. "Go then."

You stop at your room to gather supplies. You pack food and water along with your wooden club, your bow, and your quiver of arrows. As always, you wear the Nemean Lion's head and pelt.

You travel northwest, through forests of trees so tall that their branches scrape the clouds. Along the way, you stop in villages to rest and eat meals at small inns. You are not recognized, though you often hear villagers speaking of your previous battles.

For months, you camp near different brooks, streams, and freshwater ponds. King Eurystheus was right: The deer is mysterious. While many animals drink from the cool waters, none are the golden hind you're hunting.

But, at last, your patience is rewarded. You hide in the shade of a towering tree, seated on a flat boulder. Across a small clearing, there's a glint of something metallic. You scan the forest for its source.

There, emerging from behind the thick trunk of a tree is the most beautiful animal you've ever seen. It has a rack of twisting, pointed antlers that gleam gold in the sunlight. Its hide looks as smooth as velvet. And each hoof is made of deep bronze.

The deer moves to a nearby brook, looks about, then lowers its head to drink. You slowly slide down from your perch atop the boulder and draw your bow and arrow. You notch an arrow, then bring the weapon up, squeezing one eye shut and taking aim. Your hands are calm. Your breath is even.

From this distance, you are not certain that a shot will hit the beast, but any movement could startle the creature away. And if it does run, it may never return. Should you take the shot now? Or will you attempt to get closer to the hind? What will you choose to do?

To take the shot, go to page 32.

To get closer, go to page 74.

Your sword is close, but by reaching for it, you'll expose yourself to attack. There is no choice but to head for the darkness of the lion's lair.

Before the animal can pounce, you rush toward the cave. Upon reaching its shadowy interior, the stench of death and decay is overwhelming. You clap a hand over your mouth and try not to vomit. Bones snap beneath your feet. You climb atop the nearest boulder and hide.

A moment later, you hear the lion breathing. It chuffs, then issues a throaty growl. If the animal does indeed have impenetrable skin, then you will have to use your strength to defeat it.

The lion reaches your hiding place. The time to strike is now. You leap from the boulder, landing solidly atop the creature's back. Before it can shake you, you wrap your arms around its neck, tangling them in the lion's thick mane. Clasping your hands together, you squeeze the animal with all of your might.

The lion thrashes. It drives itself into the cavern wall, nearly causing you to lose your grip on it. But before long, the beast weakens. Soon enough, it falls to the earth. It closes its eyes and does not open them again.

3
The Many-Headed Monster

With your first task complete, you return to Mycenae. The pelt of the Nemean Lion is draped over your head. You burst into the throne room of King Eurystheus. The sight of you wearing the lion's head atop your own startles the king. He emits a high-pitched shriek and drops his drink to the stone floor.

"Hercules! What is this madness?" Eurystheus's voice is filled with anger.

You laugh. "I have defeated the lion as you requested. No weapon could penetrate its skin, but I discovered the animal's own claws did the trick well enough. I cut off the lion's pelt with its claws, and now I shall wear the pelt as armor."

"I see." The king waves a hand, as if to dismiss you. "From now on, leave proof of your success outside the city walls."

"As you wish, my lord." You bow. "If that is all, I will take my rest. It has been a long journey, and I have dreamed of a hot meal and a comfortable bed."

The king smiles, and you immediately dread what he is about to say. "There will be time for sleeping on Mount Olympus, if you reach it."

"Another labor? So soon?"

"Indeed. Are you familiar with the beast known as the Hydra?"

"The foul reptile that lives in the Lernean Swamps?"

"The very one."

"I've heard tales. Chop off one head, and two more grow in its place. Its blood and breath are even said to be poisonous."

In the king's eyes, there is an evil glare. The look is not unlike the glare Hera always gives you. "For your second labor," he says, "I bid you to kill the Hydra."

Again, you wonder why the all-knowing oracle sent you to this man. You bow. "As you wish."

You are given one hour to feast and prepare for your travels. Unlike the Nemean Lion, the Hydra will have to be killed with a sword. You carry the same blade as before as you leave Mycenae. You also bring with you a bow and a quiver of arrows. The lion's head and pelt still protect your head and shoulders.

As you reach the city gates, a young boy calls to you. "Hercules, wait!" It is your nephew, Iolaus. He is tall for his age and wiry, with black hair that falls to his shoulders.

You stop as he approaches.

"Is it true?" Iolaus asks. There is wonder in his eyes. "Are you traveling to slay the Hydra?"

"Aye."

"May I join you?"

You don't even think about it. "No."

"I can take you by chariot, Uncle. As you know, my family once lived near the swamps of Lernea. Take me with you, and I will lead you right to the beast's lair."

You pause to consider this. The boy makes a good argument. You could use a companion and guide, but Iolaus is still just a lad. How will he react in the heat of battle? One false move, and you could both meet your end. You must decide. Will you refuse Iolaus's offer, for his safety and for yours? Or will you bring the boy with you into the Lernean Swamps, allowing you to find the Hydra more swiftly? What will you choose to do?

To refuse Iolaus's offer, go to page 20.

To accept his offer, go to page 67.

The bird is about to disappear on the far side of the field. You cannot lose sight of it. You crash into the high grasses, swatting aside reeds.

You feel yourself begin to sink and realize that you have stepped into a marsh. It is filled with wet soil and bird droppings, masking the water beneath it. You try to stomp forward, but you can hardly lift your foot out of the muck.

In the distance, you hear a flock of birds cawing. They must be fighting over their new prey. You struggle against the muddy wasteland, but your thrashing only makes matters worse. Before long, you have sunk to your knees.

It is then that you spy one of the birds circling above you. It caws loudly to the others. Soon, birds swarm wildly in the sky.

You fumble for your bow and arrows, and you do your best to fire at the creatures. Your first shot strikes the wing of one of the birds. It drops like a stone. You are able to take out two more of the birds before they begin to dive at you. They release poisonous, metallic feathers, and you must quickly hide within the lion pelt.

You remain huddled that way for a long while, hoping the birds will cease their attack and fly away. But when you draw back the pelt and peer out at the marsh, you find the opposite to be true.

More birds have joined the others. They perch on every branch of every blackened tree along the bank of the marsh. There will be no escape this time. You have lost this battle, and your days are at an end.

Go to page 83.

As you weigh your decision, the screech of a bird echoes across the swampland. The nocturnal creature swoops above your head—so close that you feel the whisper of its wings against your face. You decide it best not to alert the forest's creatures to your presence.

"No fire," you say.

Iolaus nods and abandons the twigs and branches.

Soon, darkness drapes the forest in deep shadows. You huddle next to Iolaus at the base of a thick-trunked tree. "We will take turns keeping watch," you say as you grab your sword. "I will go first."

Your young companion does not argue. He also does not sleep. You cannot blame him.

Suddenly, you hear a soft crack, like the sound of a twig snapping. You are instantly alert.

"What is it?" Iolaus hisses in your ear. He clutches your arm, trembling.

A long shadow slithers between the trees, lit only by the soft moonlight. You cannot see what it is, but you already know the answer.

"Curses," you say. "The Hydra has found us."

The darkness makes it impossible to see anything but the creature's milky yellow eyes. When one of the Hydra's heads lunges forward, its jaws snap mere inches from your head.

"Hercules, I've been bit!" Iolaus staggers out from behind you. "I can't feel anything," he tells you before falling to the ground.

You drop to a knee beside him. Moonlight reflects off his open eyes, and your heart sinks. Iolaus is dead.

The Hydra comes at you again, and you angrily swing your sword at the beast. The serpent easily dodges. Then it coils and strikes.

The Hydra's fangs sink into your side. Its venom races through your veins. Pinpricks of pain are replaced by a cold numbness. You lose feeling in your sword arm, and the weapon drops to the ground.

When the venom reaches your legs, you topple over, landing beside your young companion. The Hydra slides in closer, and you realize with horror that this will be your final resting place.

Go to page 83.

You pluck a stone the size of your fist from a rock pile and step out from your hiding place. Holding the metal shield high above your head, you rap the stone loudly against it. The piercing sound echoes across the lake.

The birds take flight at once, turning the sky from gray to black. They swoop around, searching for the source of the noise. You draw your bow, notch an arrow, aim for the nearest bird, and take your shot.

The arrow hits its mark but only scratches the beast's metallic feathers. The scratch is enough, though, as the Hydra blood takes instant effect. The bird drops like a stone to the ground.

The rest of the flock soars toward you. You raise your shield as three of the birds release their deadly feathers. The projectiles bounce harmlessly off the metal shield with a soft clink.

It goes like this for some time, until you have slain nearly half the birds. Sensing defeat, the remaining members of the flock lift high into the air, retreating out of the land of Stymphalus forever. You have done it; Ares's pets will no longer terrorize this region.

7

The Cretan Bull

Months pass. You spend your days in the company of others, telling them of your travels. You do not see your cousin the king; he hides away in his palace.

When spring returns to Mycenae, you are visited by Copreus, the king's assistant. The plump man enters your chambers and loudly clears his throat. "Hercules," he says, his voice pinched and high. "By order of the king, I task you to your seventh labor. You will sail to the island of Crete and catch a bull given to King Minos by the god Poseidon. A ship awaits you at the port."

You have learned not to question the king, but there is often a hidden intent behind his orders. And so you prepare yourself for a great challenge.

The seaport smells of salt and fish. You spy the king's ship immediately. It is a large vessel, tended by many men. Its captain is an old, hunched-over sailor. He stands on the dock with his hands clasped behind him.

The king's ship is by far the largest vessel docked here, with two masts and dark green sails. Over a dozen oars line each side. Their flat ends are raised out of the choppy water.

The old captain approaches. "My name is Thelion," he says in a raspy voice. "Climb aboard."

You do, finding a place on the top deck as the ship's crew prepares to leave port.

For one day and night, the ship sails south toward Crete. The wind pulls the sails tight, and the ship glides smoothly across the sea.

The following afternoon, as you rest below deck, clouds gather in the sky and the sea grows angry. Towering waves lift the ship high and then bring it crashing down. It is enough to make you sea sick.

You climb above deck to see if you can help the crew. Thelion stands calmly as water splashes on each side of him. He hollers to his men, who frantically work to loosen the sails.

And then you see it. There, at the front of the ship, is a wave the size of a mountain. Standing atop the wave is a broad-shouldered man clothed in seaweed. Seashells and crabs are woven into his thick, twisting beard, and in his hands is a three-pronged trident.

"God of the Sea," you say. "Poseidon."

Suddenly, the waves around you calm. The ship is no longer tossed about. The men stop moving and stare at the god in the water.

Poseidon walks atop the sea toward the ship. He says, "Son of Zeus, do you dare to face off against the Cretan Bull?"

"I do," you shout back. You will not let the sea god frighten you.

"The creature was given to King Minos as a gift," Poseidon tells you. "When the king chose to sacrifice another bull in its place, I drove the animal mad. It must stay on Crete as the king's punishment."

"I am sorry," you say, "but I am ordered to bring it to Mycenae. I'll let no man—or god—stop me."

"We shall see about that." Poseidon turns the trident in his hands until its three prongs face the sea. Then he drives the weapon into the water. Around him, the sea begins to churn and bubble. The wind gusts again, and the ship begins to rock once more.

Behind you, Thelion shouts, "Man your stations!"

Your shipmates dash around you. The waves are fierce; they crash against the ship's hull from all sides. The craft groans and shudders under your feet. It leans to the side, and sea spray hits your face like a million cold, tiny needles.

Go to the next page.

Thelion shouts into your ear, "We cannot take much more of this! Should we change course?"

The hurricane ahead could tear the ship apart, and the captain has left the fate of the ship in your hands. Will you command them to stay on course and face Poseidon head-on? Or will you direct the ship toward calmer waters? What will you choose to do?

To continue forward, go to page 89.

To steer away from the storm, go to page 96.

You have never been to the Lernean Swamps. By yourself, you might get lost, or worse: wind up as the Hydra's next meal.

You nod your head. "You may come with me, Iolaus. But you will do as I say. Do you understand?"

"Aye," the boy responds eagerly. He dashes off to gather supplies and prepare his chariot for the journey.

The ride is long and treacherous. As you wind your way northeast, Iolaus tells stories of the Hydra. He talks of men striving to be heroes. Each entered the swamps in search of the creature—and never returned.

"It is said the great Hydra has more than twenty heads now, each with dangerous venom. One bite will paralyze a man in seconds. And the Hydra has one immortal head. It cannot be killed. So I must ask you, Hercules, how do you intend to slay this monster?"

"I will not know until I face it," you respond.

You come upon the marshes of Lernea, where you must leave the chariot behind. With Iolaus at your side, you walk among the high weeds and tall trees. A mist rises from the swamps. The stench is awful, so you take a bit of cloth and tear it in two. You pass one of the swatches to Iolaus, and you tie your own tightly across your nose and mouth.

You speak in a muffled voice. "If the Hydra's breath truly is poisonous, this might protect us."

Iolaus covers his nose and mouth, as well.

Many times, you pass thick clouds of insects. You are thankful for the cloth that protects your face.

Grotesque, black birds with large wings take flight in the distance. A coldness creeps through every pore of your body.

As the sun sets, you and your companion reach a small clearing.

"This is where the Hydra is said to live," he tells you. "But the site seems deserted."

"We will have to search out the beast," you say.

Iolaus shakes his head. "We'll only be able to see our way by moonlight. It's too dangerous to proceed."

"And yet it's too far to return to the chariot." You sit upon a large boulder and drink from your water supply. "We must camp here for the night."

Iolaus gathers small twigs and leaves. He takes a few dozen rocks and places them in a circle.

"What are you doing?" you ask.

"Starting a fire." Iolaus drops the twigs and leaves within the circle.

"No fire," you command. "It will alert the beast that we're here."

"Without it, we will be at risk from any number of creatures within the swamp," Iolaus counters. "Any of them—the Hydra included—may attack us, and we will not see it coming."

Iolaus has a point. There are many deadly creatures in the swamps of Lernea. Will you start a fire and take your chances against any beast attracted by its light? Or will you spend the night in darkness? What will you choose to do?

To light a fire, go to page 39.

To remain in the dark, go to page 59.

The crab is moving quickly across the hard-packed earth, and you know that it will kill Iolaus. So you turn from the Hydra and leap into the crab's path.

It gnashes one of its claws at you, and you knock it away with a fist. You place one foot against its ancient shell and shove the crab back toward the swamp.

The Hydra, now behind you, uses this distraction to its advantage. With one of its heads, it strikes at you.

"No!" Iolaus shouts.

His warning comes too late; the beast's jaws snap closed on you. But its venomous black fangs do not sink into your skin. The monster has struck the unbreakable hide of the Nemean Lion.

You turn your sword on the serpent and slice the head off while it's still attached to you. You shrug off the head while Iolaus burns the neck with his torch.

Returning your attention to the crab, you use your might to jump upon it, crushing its shell beneath your feet. You lift the large crab with both arms and toss it back into the swamp.

All that remains now is the Hydra's immortal head. The beast is weak and sluggish.

You walk right up to the serpent. "You fought well this night," you say, "but your days of terrorizing the people of Lernea are over." With one quick motion, you cut off the serpent's immortal head.

Unlike the other wounds, this one bleeds. You think of the rumors of the blood's poisonous quality. For a moment, you consider the idea of coating your weapons with a bit of the blood. If the rumors are true, doing so will make your arrows even more deadly. Yet at the same time, if the rumors are true, dipping your arrows is a dangerous choice to make. One false move, and the blood will poison you instead of your enemies. Is the risk worth the reward? What will you choose to do?

To dip your arrows, go to page 47.

To stay away from the blood, go to page 31.

You have enjoyed catching up with your old friend. And it would be wise to remain in the cave overnight, sleeping on a bed of straw instead of the cold ground.

As the celebration continues, a gift is wheeled into the cave by Brom. He rolls it directly to Pholus. "A gift given to us by Dionysus, the god of the grape harvest," he says.

Pholus opens the gift, and immediately you know something is wrong. A thin, scented vapor begins to fill the cavern. You cover your mouth with one hand as the others inhale the foul odor.

"Pholus, close the gift," you say. "Now!"

But Pholus cannot hear you. He is watching as two centaurs across the cave begin to fight one another. Their swords clash.

You grasp Pholus firmly and shake him. "It's driving them mad!" you cry.

You place the lid atop the box, but the damage is done. Friends turn against one another. Brom, spear in hand, gallops toward you. You quickly dive to the dirt to dodge his attack.

This was no gift from Dionysus. This is the work of someone else.

"Hera," you whisper.

As if you've summoned her, Hera emerges from the vapors. She wears an evil smile.

You draw your sword and rush toward her. But the goddess vanishes. Was she ever there, or has the madness reached you, too?

"You brought this evil into our home!" Pholus shouts behind you.

You spin to face him. "Pholus, this is the work of Hera, not me."

Pholus lifts his sword, and before you can defend yourself, he uses it against you. Pain radiates through your body. You find it hard to breathe. You drop your sword and fall to your knees.

You think of Mount Olympus, of the immortality you will never know, and your eyes drift shut.

Go to page 83.

You are no great archer, and to shoot the deer from this distance, you would need perfect aim. So you slowly move forward, taking great care with every step. You keep your eyes on the creature. It continues to drink from the brook, unaware of your presence.

That's when you think back to King Eurystheus's request. He asked you to fetch the hind, not to kill the animal. A tricky bit of wordplay; it seems your cousin wishes you to fail.

You are too wrapped in your thoughts to notice a small twig before you. You step on it and it cracks, a quiet, brittle sound.

The hind's head snaps up. It alertly looks back and forth. Its muscles tense. Then it leaps over the brook with one majestic bound.

You quickly choose a clean arrow, notch it, raise your bow, and take aim. However, you aim not for the animal's heart but for its back legs.

As the hind lands on the far side of the water, you release the arrow. The dart finds its way between the deer's back legs. The arrow trips the creature, and the deer falls to the ground.

It remains still for some time. You run across the clearing, through the brook, and onto the other side. The animal's chest rises and falls. The hind is alive; you have only dazed it.

You grasp the creature's antlers and lift it from the ground. It is heavy, but you hoist the unconscious deer over your shoulders with ease.

"How dare you?" The voice comes from behind.

Suddenly, the forest is alive with activity. Trees sway back and forth, and the wind howls. You turn to find a beautiful woman standing near you. She is young, tall, and clothed in a green dress and hunting boots. Her brown hair is pulled back and held in place by a crown made of leaves. A golden bow is slung over one shoulder. She is the goddess of the hunt.

"Artemis," you gasp, as the deer falls from your shoulders, back to the earth.

"Hercules," Artemis says.

"You know my name?"

Artemis nods. "You look like your father, although Zeus is a bit taller. Now explain why you are hunting my prize animal!"

"I did not know the deer belonged to you," you say.

"A creature this beautiful? This unique? How could it not belong to a goddess?"

"I should have known," you admit "You have my apologies, Artemis. I am enslaved by King Eurystheus and was asked to bring him the deer. I wish the animal no harm."

Artemis stares at you with hazel eyes. You did not realize the gaze of a goddess could be so frightening.

"If I allow you to take the deer to the king," she says, "do I have your word that you'll release it unharmed?"

You do not hesitate to answer. "You have my word."

Artemis nods. "Go, then. Complete your task. And when I see you again, I wish it to be at your father's side on Mount Olympus."

"As do I." You lift the animal once more onto your shoulders and say, "Thank you, Artemis."

But the goddess has already disappeared.

5
The Great Boar

Eurystheus's smile as you enter his palace is wicked. "You have returned," he says, "and it seems you have killed the poor creature."

You lay the hind on the marble floor before the throne. Even lying down, the creature's golden antlers stretch high above your head. Eurystheus sees the deer's chest rise and fall evenly, and his smile fades.

"My lord, you tasked me to fetch the animal, not kill it," you say. "And so I have."

The king turns his back on you, his fists clenched.

"The golden deer belongs to the goddess Artemis," you continue. "Did you know this, cousin? I fear that you are trying to trick me."

Without turning back, King Eurystheus says, "On Mount Erymanthus, there is a mighty boar. It is a beast far more dangerous than an ordinary wild pig. Bring it to me."

You feel the need to clarify. "Alive?"

There is a long silence. Then the king responds. "Yes."

"As you wish." You kneel before the deer and place your hand on the creature's velvet fur. The deer's ear twitches. Its head lifts from the cold floor, and it gazes at you with almond-colored eyes. Then it rises, its hooves clipping across the marble floor.

You lead the animal out of the palace. Townspeople stare as you pass. Outside the city, you give the deer one last pat upon its back and whisper, "Return to Artemis."

The hind quickly bounds away. With a glimmer from its golden antlers, it disappears into the nearest copse of trees. You doubt it will ever be seen again.

As you prepare for your next labor, the weather grows cold. You pack extra tunics and skins for your journey to Mount Erymanthus.

For many days, you walk north. The bitter wind cuts across your face, and you bundle yourself warmly.

The territory of Arcadia is known as the land of the centaurs, a race of creatures with the upper torso of a human and the hindquarters of a horse. One of them, the great advisor Pholus, is your friend.

It has been a long time since you've seen Pholus, and your friend is always full of wisdom. Perhaps he will know something that will help you capture the boar. You turn from Mount Erymanthus and head down the winding dirt road leading to Mount Pelion, where Pholus lives.

Mount Pelion is steep and thickly forested. As you follow its dirt path, you search for signs of the centaurs—trampled grass or hoof prints—but find nothing.

You pass an outcropping of rocks, and a voice booms, "Halt! Who goes there?"

You raise your hands to show the newcomer you mean no harm. "I seek Pholus," you say, turning around.

Standing behind you is a young centaur. He holds a long, thin sword, and it is pointed right at you.

"Why do you seek him?" the centaur asks sternly.

"Stand down, Brom," says a second voice. From behind the trees trots Pholus, a centaur with a hide of silver and gray hair that hangs to his shoulders. Your old mentor looks well.

Brom, the eager centaur, lowers his sword.

As the centaurs lead you farther into the forest, you speak of your adventures. Before long, you reach a cave entrance hidden by vines and leaves.

Inside, the cave opens into a space lit with many torches. It is a centaur camp. Many of the creatures sleep or eat. Pholus motions to a nearby table. You sit, while Pholus lowers himself to the dirt floor.

"Why have you come to me, Hercules?" he asks.

"For my newest labor, King Eurystheus has sent me to capture the Erymanthian Boar."

"That old thing? Ugly. Smells of rot. You can have him," Pholus says. "But beware. That boar may be even stronger than you. The simplest way to defeat the beast is to let the boar defeat itself."

"Have you taken to riddles now, Pholus?" you ask. "That seems unlike you."

"No, no," Pholus says. "A beast such as that cannot keep up with a man as fit as you. Lead it on a chase, up and down the mountainside. It will fall over from exhaustion without you ever laying a hand on it."

It is good advice, and you are glad to have taken this small detour.

"Now," Pholus says loudly so the other centaurs can hear, "we shall dine with the son of Zeus!"

At once, the others dash about in preparation for a kingly meal.

When your belly is filled, you know that a decision must be made. It is nearly nightfall, and a safe choice is to stay with the centaurs until morning. Yet you know that the sooner you begin your hunt, the better your chances of finding the boar's trail. So, should you stay or should you go? What will you choose to do?

To stay with the centaurs, go to page 72.

To leave now, go to page 10.

Today has already been strange and scary. The last thing you need is a haunted book. There's no way you're taking that thing off the shelf.

Instead, you get to your feet, crouch low, and look for a new place in the library to hide. Ms. Englehopper, the librarian, spies you.

"Excuse me, young man," she says.

You stop in your tracks.

"Is there something I can help you find?" she asks.

"No, I don't think so," you grumble.

With slumped shoulders, you walk away. Part of you wonders if the book could have helped you somehow. But you'll never know.

For now, you'll hide in the library until you're sure that Tyler isn't waiting anymore. Maybe someday you'll be brave enough to stand up to him. But today is not that day.

Go to the next page.

The End

Try Again

You watch as the sun creeps lower. It will soon be dark, and the ship will be a perfect target.

"We'll go ashore," you say.

You divide the ship's men, taking with you a team of strong swordsmen. Thelion and the others will remain with the ship.

You lead the men down the dock and onto the forest trail. The group stays close together, with weapons drawn. The path winds higher and higher, until you think you cannot climb any more.

As you reach level ground, you begin to hear sounds of combat. There is a clearing ahead where flickering firelight dances off the trees. When you reach the edge of the trees, you see it is an Amazon camp.

Large stones line the far side of the clearing. Metal bowls, filled with fire, light the camp. In the middle of the clearing, a number of Amazons appear to be training. They combat each other, one on one, with long spears. A circle of onlookers watches closely.

You see the three females who met you at the ship. They are speaking to a tall woman with raven-colored hair and a golden cloak about her shoulders. On her head is a crown, and around her wrists are large, golden bracelets. It's Queen Hippolyte.

"Do not move," a voice hisses in your ear. The cool metal of a spear touches your throat. A small group of Amazons stand behind you and your companions.

The Amazons push you into the clearing and then onto your knees. The training exercise comes to a halt, and Queen Hippolyte draws her weapon. Under her cloak, you spy a glint of gold. She is wearing the belt you seek.

The queen says, "You were told to remain on board your ship."

"My apologies, Queen Hippolyte," you reply. "I only wish to speak with you. I have been sent by King Eurystheus to ask for your golden belt."

The queen's hand goes to her waist. She draws her cloak over the belt.

"He lies!" shouts an Amazon standing among the training warriors. She has wavy brown hair pulled back and looks shockingly like—*Hera?*

"They've come to kidnap the queen!" the Amazon continues. She begins to rile up the others.

Around her, the warriors arm themselves.

"Your Majesty," you say. "This is nonsense. Please, hear me out."

"Rise," the queen says. She points her sword at your own. "If you want my belt, you will have to take it."

You do not wish to fight the queen, but it's now your only hope.

With a loud battle cry, the Amazons attack.

Your companions draw their swords and fight off the warrior women as best they can. The queen swings her sword at you in a wide arc. She is fast; you barely block her stroke.

You match Queen Hippolyte blow for blow, your swords dancing. She is a strong fighter. It has been a long while since you had a challenge like this.

Finally, you see an opening and swing your sword down upon her. The blow glances off the queen's sword, knocking her to one knee. She is dazed, and her belt is exposed. With one quick move, it could be yours.

You drop your weapon, grasp the belt with both hands, and steal it off the queen. "I'm sorry," you say. Then, rising, you cry out, "Men, retreat!"

You tuck the belt beneath your arm and race for the jungle path. Your companions hurry to catch up.

Amazons hurl their spears at you. One slices past your left ear. Another strikes the man to your right, knocking him to the ground.

Night has covered the jungle in shadows. You cannot see where you're going. You step off the path and plunge deeper into the jungle. You hear the Amazons at your back.

The going is tough, and more than once you slip and nearly drop the golden belt. You find the path again and press onward. It leads sharply down, and you know the seashore is near.

Suddenly, you hear the faint sound of voices and shouting. As you burst from the jungle onto the shore, your heart falls.

Thelion's ship is in flames. The Amazons have beaten you to the docks. They have captured the sailors.

The Amazons see you, and you are soon surrounded. You drop the golden belt into the sand.

One of the Amazons places a pair of heavy metal cuffs about your wrists. She says, "They were forged by

Hephaestus, blacksmith of the gods, and they are strong enough to hold a Titan."

It is true; try as you might, you cannot break free from these bonds.

The Amazons lead you and the sailors back into the dark jungle. Here you will spend the remainder of your days as their prisoner, living deep within a cave, never seeing the sunlight again.

Go to page 83.

Thelion waits for your decision. Your eyes are on Poseidon, who stands atop the angry water.

"Forward!" you shout.

Thelion gives your command, and the ship continues to move into the storm, heading right for the sea god.

Poseidon does not move. Behind him, a massive wave rises, the largest one yet. You notice with growing fear that the wave is shaped like a sea serpent. It lifts higher into the sky, until it nearly blocks out the storm clouds. You brace yourself for impact, and it smashes into the ship.

You hear the ship splinter but hold. Waves pound the ship's hull from all sides. Water splashes onto the deck, washing nearly a half-dozen men overboard. You fear you've made the wrong choice. This is the end.

And then, as swiftly as the storm began, it ends. The waves shrink to small whitecaps. The storm clouds part, and a shaft of sunlight filters through. Your shipmates quickly throw netting into the water, hoping to save those swept overboard.

Poseidon nods and says, "You are brave, Hercules. I will admit that."

"I will not back down," you say. "If I am to reach my goal of immortality, I must bring the bull to the king."

There is a long silence. Then Poseidon nods. "So be it," he says. "Bring no harm to the animal, and it is yours. Safe winds, son of Zeus."

You bow before the god. As you do, the wind grows strong again. This time, it is at your back.

In two days, you reach Crete. The island is lush, with high mountains and sandy beaches. A royal gathering greets you at the docks, including King Minos.

"You're here for my bull?" the king asks.

You take a knee in the sand. "Yes, my lord."

"As beautiful as it is, the beast tramples the earth and attacks my people. I will gladly be rid of it."

King Minos leads you to a waiting chariot led by two white horses. You take your place beside the king as the driver commands the horses. The chariot winds its way along the shoreline.

Soon, the land appears battered. Trees are upturned and grasses laid flat. In the distance, you see the king's bull. It is running across the white sand. As you get closer, you see that its hide is the color of the ocean, and its horns and hooves are made of coral and shells. One side of the beast is covered in barnacles.

You leap from the chariot and cross the sand. When the bull sees you, it flares its nostrils and drives its back hoof into the ground.

The bull is about to charge, so you must decide the best way to fight. Will you utilize your speed in attacking the slower animal? Or should you rely upon your super-strength in battling this powerful creature? What will you choose to do?

To attack with speed, go to page 134.

To use your strength, go to page 125.

If you want Prometheus to offer you information, you need to earn his trust. There is only one way to do this. You must free the trickster from his shackles.

You continue upward, climbing the sheer cliff. The eagle dives at you, coming so close that it nearly knocks you down the mountain.

The second time it does this, though, you're ready. As it reaches its razor-sharp talons for you, you swing your sword, striking the bird in the chest. It suddenly drops from the sky, twisting and twirling out of sight far below.

You sheath your sword and continue climbing up the mountain.

Soon, you are near enough to hear Prometheus. He strains against his bonds. "Whoever you are," he says, his voice a croaking whisper, "I thank you."

"I'm glad to do it," you say. "My name is Hercules, and I seek knowledge from you."

Prometheus looks puzzled. "From me? What can I offer? I have been bound to this mountain for years."

You explain that you're searching for the lost garden. As you do, you break the chains at his wrists and ankles.

"I see," he says, touching the raw, red skin on his wrists. "I do not know the answer to your question. However, I know what you must do next. Do you know who the Hesperidins' father is?"

You shake your head.

"Perhaps the name Atlas?" he asks.

You know this name. Atlas is the son of a Titan. He's been punished, like Prometheus. Atlas must bear the weight of the heavens on his shoulders for all eternity.

"Atlas is their father?" you exclaim.

"Yes, and he is also my brother."

Again, you are surprised.

Prometheus tells you where to find his brother, and together the two of you descend the mountain. You bid the trickster farewell and begin your search for his brother.

Your quest leads you far to the west and south of Mount Caucasus, to a land known as Hesperia. There, you find Atlas standing atop a great mountain. He is a large man, the size of a Titan, and the heavens rest on his great shoulders. You see his muscles straining at the burden.

"Who goes there?" Atlas's voice booms.

"Hercules, son of Zeus," you say.

"If you wish to get in my good graces, boy, I would suggest not using that title."

You have forgotten. It was your father who punished Atlas with this burden.

Atlas continues. "What does the son of the dreaded Lord Thunderbolt wish of me?"

You tell Atlas of your journey so far and ask him for the garden's location.

"I will do better than tell you," Atlas answers. "I will go there for you and bring back the apples. You need only take my place."

"I cannot," you say. "I must fetch them myself."

"And by doing so, you would anger my daughters. I have seen what my daughters can do when they are upset. There is a reason Hera trusts them to protect her cherished garden."

You shake your head. "Even if I were to accept your offer, I cannot hold the heavens on my shoulders."

"Oh, I am certain you can. Allow me to fetch the apples for you. I will be back before you know it."

If what Atlas says is true, then the battle you will face in the garden shall be great—perhaps impossible. Yet can you trust Atlas to return with the apples? If he doesn't, you'll be stuck holding the heavens in his place, forever. You must decide. What will you choose to do?

To trust Atlas, go to page 148.

To get the apples yourself, go to page 143.

The ship cracks around you. Thelion is right: It cannot take much more of this.

"Steer west!" you shout.

Thelion gives your command, and the ship suddenly lurches away from Poseidon and his angry storm.

There is a horrible noise from within the water, like the angry howl of a sea serpent. The ship shudders and comes to a sudden stop. Sailors topple onto the deck and are washed overboard.

You ask Thelion, "What's happened?"

"A rock has torn open the hull," he shouts.

The deck swarms with men. They tear off planks of wood and grab handfuls of food and bread. Then, not wanting to be lost with the ship, they leap into the sea.

You leap overboard, too. Then you watch as the ship sinks below the surface.

You try hard to glimpse Poseidon, but the sea god has abandoned you to your fate. Like the men treading water around you, the sea will soon become your final resting place.

Go to page 83.

The queen is stunned; the belt is within your grasp. Yet you fear the two Amazons with torches will destroy the whole ship. You quickly turn from Queen Hippolyte and advance on the newcomers.

Aside from the torches, they are unarmed. One tries to swipe at you with the blazing fire, and it singes the edge of the lion pelt on your back. You snatch the torch from her hand and fling it into the sea.

The second Amazon tries to flee from you, but she stumbles and drops the torch. With one swift kick from you, the second torch joins the first in the water.

With the threat of fire gone, you return your focus to Queen Hippolyte. And just in time.

She swings her sword, and you swiftly raise yours. The two blades hum as they clash.

The ship sways as it heads for open water, and it is hard to keep your balance. Around you, some of your shipmates fall. Others force the remaining Amazon warriors off the craft and into the sea. Soon, only the queen is left.

The ship lurches and the queen stops to regain her balance. It is the opening you're waiting for. You do not wish to kill the queen. Instead, you drop your sword to the deck and run at her. As you collide, you wrap your arms around her. Together, you crash into the wooden rail at the edge of the ship and fall overboard.

Hippolyte struggles against you, but you do not let go. Tangled as one, you roll and turn in the sea, until it is hard to tell which way is up.

You are a skilled swimmer, and you do not panic. With one hand, you unfasten the golden belt from the queen's waist and take it as your own.

You release the queen and kick for the surface. When your head emerges from the water, you gulp a breath of crisp air. The ship is not far. You swim for it. Some of the men aboard see you and throw a net for you to grab.

Queen Hippolyte surfaces near the docks. Instead of chasing after you, she swims for the shore. Her fellow Amazons help her to dry land.

As you climb the net to safety, you call out into the darkness, "My apologies, Queen Hippolyte! I wish it had not happened this way!"

Though your labor is complete, you have made yourself the enemy of a very powerful band of warriors.

9

Geryon and His Cattle

When you present the belt to King Eurystheus's daughter, she squeals with delight. The princess dons her gift and rushes to a mirror to marvel at its beauty.

The king seems pleased. "You have done well," he says. "I wish that I could reward you for your work." He continues. "Alas, my kingdom is running short of cattle, and legend tells of a herd of cattle unlike any other."

"Let me guess, cousin. For my next labor, you wish me to bring them back for you."

"Correct," King Eurystheus says

You nod and then leave, allowing the king and his daughter to admire the new belt in peace.

Once again, you are in need of Thelion's ship and crew. The cattle are far across the Mediterranean Sea on an island called Erytheia. It is your adventure's most distant destination, and Thelion fears the ship's hold will not carry all of your supplies and the cattle. Nevertheless, you must journey onward.

The ship is at sea for months. But at long last, you reach the island you seek. There's no port, so Thelion and his crew sail the ship into a small cove, where it runs ashore. You leap from the ship and swiftly head off to search for the cattle.

You find a well-worn path in the woods and follow it until you reach a grand pasture. Dozens of cows dot the landscape. They are huge beasts, almost as large as the Cretan Bull. Near the pasture is an enormous stone farmhouse. It seems that, once again, King Eurystheus has tricked you: Geryon, the cattle's owner, is a giant.

Go to the next page.

Loud snoring comes from inside the home. And if Geryon is sleeping, then it's the perfect moment to seize the animals. With any luck, you can be gone before he wakes. But should you check the home to make sure he's sleeping? Or will doing so be a waste of time that might get you caught? What will you choose to do?

To check the house, go to page 106.

To take the cattle, go to page 132.

It's too dangerous to climb any farther. You will talk with Prometheus from where you are.

You slide your sword into its sheath and grasp the cliff with both hands. "Prometheus!" you call out.

He does not seem to hear you at first. You shout his name again, louder. The eagle, now riled, lands on a nearby mountain peak and watches.

Prometheus turns his head to you. When he speaks, his voice is nothing more than a whispering croak. You must strain to hear him.

"Who are you?" he asks.

"My name is Hercules, and I seek the garden of the Hesperides. Do you know where I might find it?"

Prometheus is silent a long while. Then he laughs, a short bark that makes him cough. "I have been hanging here . . . for nearly thirty years," he says. "And you . . . expect me to tell you what you'd like to hear . . . simply because you climbed up to see me?"

You must do something to earn Prometheus's trust. "Ask, and I shall help however I can," you say.

"Free me," the chained man says. "Get me off this rock, and I'll tell you what you need to know."

"It is done." You begin to climb again.

As you do, the eagle takes flight. It must have been listening and now knows your plan—a foolish error on your part.

The eagle dives toward you. You reach for your sword, holding on to the stone with one hand. The rock crumbles, though, and you lose your grip.

Downward you fall. The ground seems to rush up to meet you. You crash against it with a tremendous thud. It is the last sound you ever hear.

Go to page 83.

Nothing is as it seems in the Underworld, not even the man Charon. You don't trust him. Maybe it's the way his eyes burn red in the darkness. He is evil—and you know it.

You shake your head. "I'll find another way," you tell him.

"There is no other way into the Underworld," says Charon. His raspy voice sounds like metal dragged across stone. "You must cross the River Styx to get to its gates."

You think about the other cave and the secrets it holds. "Your service is not needed," you proclaim.

"Very well," he says. As fast as a blink, he is gone.

The new cave is dark, but you hear the sound of rushing water and are sure it is the River Styx. You hold your club and step carefully into the darkness.

After walking down a slight slope and around a pile of fallen rocks, you reach the banks of the River Styx. It looks similar to the spot where you saw Charon. You glance to your right, half-expecting to see the ferry-man—or another like him—waiting for you.

No one is there.

Curious, you begin to walk along the riverbank. Surely, there will be another place to cross.

The river snakes along, and you follow beside it. You stop once to rest and gaze into the black water. You are startled to see faces peering back at you. Lost souls. You hope that you will not become one of them.

After a time, you admit defeat, realizing that there is no other way across the river. You try to retrace your steps. It should be easy; there is only one river, one path to take. And yet you do not come across the cave.

You wander back and forth for hours, days, months, and even years. This is where you remain, lost in the darkness of the Underworld, listening to the moans of unseen ghosts.

You explore the banks of the River Styx for more than a hundred years—until you give up and become just another soul that calls the Underworld home.

Go to page 83.

You can never be too careful. Despite the awful snoring sounds drifting from the farmhouse, you decide to get a closer look.

Keeping low to the ground, you sneak to a window carved in the stone. The snoring grows louder as you reach the house. The stench coming from inside the building is disgustingly strong.

You peer into the dark window. Geryon is one of the ugliest creatures you've ever seen. He has three bodies that are joined at the waist. His skin is gray and scaled. Bits of it flake off with each rise and fall of his three chests. The giant is lying on a bed of straw.

You also spy a second mound of straw in the corner. It is not as massive as Geryon's bed, but it is quite large. The giant must own a pet.

You hear an animal approaching, and you duck into the thick shrubs. From near the pasture, a dog with two heads comes forth. It has black and white fur, and wide paws. You fear it will catch your scent, but the ugly beast proceeds into the house.

You run to the pasture and throw open the gate. The cattle are spooked, but soon you are able to gather the herd. You lead them, side by side, in a long trail back through the woods.

When you reach the ship, Thelion's eyes grow wide. "There's no way they'll all fit," he says.

"Then we'll take what we can," you respond.

Four of Thelion's men help to lead the cattle into the ship's hold. As you prepare to board, a mighty roar bends the trees and shakes the earth at your feet. Geryon has awoken, and two-dozen cattle still remain on the sandy shore.

"Leave the rest," you shout. "Push off, and make for open water. Don't worry about me. See that the ship is safe."

You turn back to the path in time to see Geryon's dog burst into the clearing. The dog sees you and races forward. You cannot escape, so you must attack.

To fight with your club, go to page 140.

To fight with your bow and arrows, go to page 146.

Cerberus wishes to attack, but you will respond with kindness. You muster up every bit of courage within you, and you stand your ground. When the hound reaches you, you take the opportunity to leap onto its back, wrapping your arms about its middle neck, much like you did with the Nemean Lion.

Cerberus's other heads twist and snap at you, but you are beyond their reach. Squeezing with all your might, you speak into the dog's ear. "I do not wish to harm you," you tell it. "Come with me, and you'll be safe. Do you understand?"

Go to the next page.

For a moment, the dog continues to thrash about. Then, slowly, it lowers and sits. You release your grip on its neck, waiting for it to attack. It does not.

You walk around and face the canine's three heads. Cerberus growls. You reach out one hand, and the beast lowers its head until your palm is against its muzzle.

"Thank you," you say.

When you turn to face the River Styx, Charon is there, waiting for you. His boat appears to have grown. It is now large enough for you and Cerberus to safely climb aboard.

Soon, you're making your way out of the Underworld with its guardian at your side.

12
A Visit from Zeus

Upon returning to Mycenae with Cerberus, you let the canine do as he pleases. The three-headed monster runs through the king's castle, frightening Eurystheus so much that he hides and shouts, "You are free, cousin! Go! Leave my city and never return!"

"Gladly!" You whistle for Cerberus, and together you put Mycenae at your back for good.

Freedom is a wonderful thing. You bravely fought each beast that Hera placed before you, and you've come out stronger. That is the thing about bravery, which you now understand. Although fear and danger take many forms, so too does bravery. It is how you handle each trial that matters.

You guide Cerberus back to the stones of Taenarum. The hound quickly vanishes within the rocky cavern.

The sky darkens. Lightning streaks above you. In its wake stands the god Zeus. He is broad-shouldered, draped in white, with a beard to match. In one hand, he holds the crackling energy of a lightning bolt.

"You have been quite busy, my son," he says.

"Each task placed before me, I completed. I am ready to take my place on Mount Olympus."

Zeus places a hand on your shoulder. "Soon," he says. "There are still many adventures left for you. But remain strong. Remain brave. When you finally tire and need a place to rest, Mount Olympus will be waiting for you. I will be waiting for you, my son."

You close your eyes and imagine what it will be like to spend eternity on Mount Olympus. The people of Greece will share stories of your labors for centuries to come. Your name will become linked to courage and to bravery.

Someday, you think. *Someday.*

Go to page 156.

The ferryman was clear: Do not step from the path. Whatever Hades has sent your way, it is a test. And you must not fail. So you stand your ground and hold your club, though it will do no good against them.

The lost souls are just feet from you now. Their hands are outstretched, reaching for you. Their moans echo throughout the enclosed space. The sound gives you goose bumps. You cannot help but be afraid.

"Begone!" A female voice pierces the air.

The ghosts scatter. Many dissolve to nothing, while the rest disappear into the stone walls.

A woman stands before you. She is tall and thin, with golden hair that is almost white. A cape hangs from her shoulders, and in her hand is a scepter.

"Persephone," you say, bowing. The woman before you is the queen of the Underworld and Hades's wife.

Persephone motions for you to rise. "It is not often they hear the sound of a heartbeat," she says. "That is what drew them to you. Now, come."

She leads you along the path, past the cave where you saw the throne room. Now, nothing is there but darkness.

Soon you reach the end of the tunnel. It opens onto a cavern so grand that you cannot see its ceiling. Before you is a narrow stone staircase leading up. Around it on all sides is the black water of the River Styx. High above is the throne of King Hades.

Persephone leads you up the steep stairs. You must watch your step. One wrong move and you'll fall to the cold waters below.

At the top, you find Hades seated on a throne made of rocks, bone, and skulls. "My dear nephew Hercules," he says, "to what do we owe the pleasure?"

You tell him of the prize you seek.

"Cerberus?" Hades laughs. "This deed sounds more like your queen mother's doing than the meek king of Mycenae."

You nod. "It is."

"You know I loathe Hera as much as she loathes you," he confesses.

"Yes, Lord Hades."

"So you came all this way, into the heart of the dead, to complete an impossible task. I say, Hercules, there is something about you that I rarely see down here:

courage. You may take the hound to your king. But use no weapons against him, and return him unharmed."

"Thank you, my lord."

You carefully descend the stairs and travel back along the torch-lit tunnel. You reach its end without meeting any lost souls, and you find Cerberus awake and alert. It is almost as if he knew you were coming.

Cerberus growls and barks, a deep sound that fills the darkness. You grip your club. Then, remembering Hades's words, you place the club on the cave floor.

Cerberus pounces, swiping at you with one of its huge paws. The blow knocks you from your feet. You are dazed but you quickly rise. The hound does not wait for you to steady yourself. It snaps its jaws. Just before they close, you wheel back, narrowly avoiding death.

Cerberus turns its head to the left, knocking you sideways. You fly through the air and hit the stone wall hard. Cerberus is far stronger than you imagined.

You stagger to your feet.

The hound watches you as it crouches low, waiting to pounce again. Then Cerberus charges.

This moment could very well change the tide of the fight in your favor. The beast's hasty attack has left him open to a solid punch, which could lead to your victory. Yet at its heart, this monster is nothing more than an oversized dog. Perhaps you can befriend it and end the fight in peace. You must decide quickly. What will you choose to do?

To attack Cerberus, go to page 130.

To try taming Cerberus, go to page 108.

Dropping to one knee, you set the club in the sand and draw out the bow. From the quiver you draw one of the special arrows. You notch it into the string, pull back, and aim for Geryon.

With a soft *thwack*, you release the bow. The arrow sings through the sky and strikes the giant directly in the throat of its center head.

For a moment, Geryon seems unfazed. You begin to fear that the giant is too large to be affected by the Hydra poison. Then he stumbles and staggers. A look of surprise crosses all three of his faces.

Like a mighty tree, Geryon falls. When the giant hits the ground, sand, dirt, trees, boulders, and even cattle shake. You are forced backward, into the sea, where waves churn as they would in a violent storm.

Far off in the sea, Thelion's ship rocks and fights against the hurricane-like waves. You dive beneath the water and swim as fast as you can to catch them.

The water calms before you reach the ship. You enjoy a quiet, safe voyage home.

10
The Garden of
the Golden Apples

Months pass, and you hear nothing from the king.
You wonder if Hera is behind his decisions, sending you
on tasks and hoping you'll fail. You are almost certain
she is to blame.

Then one day, you receive a scroll from the king,
demanding your immediate presence.

Copreus greets you at the palace door and leads you
to the king. Eurystheus is seated upon his throne, eating
a beautiful red apple.

"Do you know of the garden watched over by the
Hesperides?" he asks. "The Hesperides are powerful
women who protect the garden with their lives."

"I have heard tales," you say, "but few people know

its location."

"Well, I would like you to find it and bring back a handful of the golden apples that grow there."

You cannot help but laugh. "Those apples were given to Hera by my father, and she will never let me steal them from her. I'm sorry, but this task is impossible."

"Yet I know you will find a way to do it." Eurystheus descends the steps and begins to leave. "Bring me the apples, cousin. I command it."

You sigh and say, "As you wish, my lord."

You begin your task at once. It isn't easy to search for a place that a goddess does not wish to be found. You wander the world for many months, through deserts, over mountains, and across the seas.

In a village on the Aegean Sea, your luck turns. You wander through a market that smells of fish, salt, and cooked vegetables.

An old man seated near a mud-brick building says, "You appear lost."

"I've been searching for something for a very long time," you tell him.

"The garden of the Hesperides."

You're surprised. How does this man know this?

The elderly man sees your puzzled expression and smiles. "Nothing escapes the Old Man of the Sea."

"Nereus." The man before you is the eldest son of the Earth and Sea.

"If it is indeed the garden you seek, then I can lead you in the right direction," Nereus says. "Only I and the trickster Prometheus know where to find it."

Your hopes rise. "Where is it?"

"I will tell you—if you can catch me."

Before your eyes, the old man seems to shed his skin. He changes into a long, winding serpent. He slithers quickly through the market.

You chase after Nereus until you reach the docks. The old man plans to disappear into the sea.

You run faster, your legs and lungs burning. Just as the serpent is about to slide into the water, you reach out and grasp its tail. It whips about, fighting to be free. But you won't let it slip away.

The snake transforms into a snapping crab. You hold fiercely to Nereus until he turns back into an old man.

"Well done, Hercules," he says. "When last I heard,

the garden of the Hesperides was in the north, along the shores of the Gaian Sea."

"Are you certain?" you ask.

"No. My memory, it drifts."

Nereus has been honored among the gods for an eternity. His word should be trusted. But still, you cannot shake the feeling in your stomach, the one telling you not to believe the old man.

You release your grip, and the old man drops to the sand. "I'm sorry," you say. "I cannot trust your word."

Nereus says nothing. He simply transforms back into the sea serpent you chased through the market and slithers into the water, out of sight. You know without a doubt that you will never see the old man again.

You leave the seaside village in search of the trickster Prometheus. You know exactly where to find him.

You head north to a range of mountains. There, you find Mount Caucasus, where Zeus has chained Prometheus for mocking the gods. Each day, an eagle swoops down and pecks out his liver. When the eagle is gone, Prometheus's liver grows back, only to be taken by the eagle the following day.

After climbing for about an hour, you spy thick chains emerging from a sheer cliff face. Looking up, you see Prometheus standing on a thin ledge of stone. The chains bind his wrists and ankles.

As you climb, you spot the eagle. It swoops low and snaps at you with its talons. You draw your sword, but it's hard to climb the mountain with just one hand.

Reaching Prometheus will be difficult, and you will have to fight off the dangerous eagle. Yet if you call out to Prometheus, he might not trust you enough to speak with you. Which is the wiser choice? Continue climbing the mountain, or speak with Prometheus from there? What will you choose to do?

To keep climbing, go to page 92.

To call to Prometheus, go to page 102.

The cave to your left may hold any kind of danger. With the ferryman Charon, at least you know what you're up against.

You nod to the ancient figure. "I will go with you."

He points toward the rickety craft. You climb aboard and take a seat on a plank. A single oar made of bone rests beside you. Charon joins you. His extra weight does not make the craft tilt or rock. He picks up the oar and pushes off from the riverbank.

Charon doesn't make any sound as you cross the River Styx. You glance down at the black water and are shocked to see faces staring back at you. Your heart leaps into your throat. Hands seem to reach for the water's surface, trying to grab at the passing boat.

"Are those . . ." you begin to ask.

"Good, bad, every soul finds its way to the Underworld," is Charon's response.

When you reach the far riverbank, you exit the boat as quickly as possible. There is but one cave here. On either side of the cave is a gate made of bone. The path is well lit, with torches hanging from bone lanterns along each wall.

Lying near the cave is Cerberus, the three-headed dog. He is thick-muscled, with black fur and jaws filled with huge teeth. The beast does not attack but gives a deep growl from each of its throats.

You think of snatching the canine now and asking Charon to take you back. But Hades will never let you leave the Underworld without his permission. You must return for the hound later.

Charon says, "You will find Lord Hades at the far end of the cave. Do not leave the path."

You do as he says, walking through the bone gates and into the stone cavern. Once, you look back, but Charon is no longer at the riverbank. Cerberus watches you closely.

The cave doesn't appear to end, and you walk for what seems like hours. There is a soft sound behind you.

You grasp the club at your side and turn. Standing not ten feet away is a man. He is ghostly pale. When he steps forward, he seems to glide across the stone. Another of Hades's trapped souls.

You cannot fight him, so you quicken your speed. A second soul joins the first, a woman. Soon, more lost souls follow. Their ranks clog the passage at your back and force you forward.

And then you see a soul coming toward you from the path ahead: a great beast not unlike the Nemean Lion. It pads forward, blocking the way.

You're trapped. The ghosts have you surrounded.

Ahead to your right, off the path, there is a break in the cave. Is that the throne of Hades you see? And is it the god of the Underworld himself, seated upon it?

You recall Charon saying that you must not leave the path. But Hades's throne room is before you, and the ghosts are pressing in from both sides. Nothing is as it seems here, not even Charon. You don't trust him. He seems evil.

Will you take Charon's advice? Or should you step off the path? What will you choose to do?

To stay on the path, go to page 112.

To step off the path, go to page 141.

The beast is strong, but you trust in the fact that you are even stronger. The bull lowers its horns and runs toward you, kicking up sand with each step.

As it nears, the bull lowers its head and leads with its twisting horns. You hold out your hands and grab them.

The beast collides with you, sending a shiver of pain through your body. Your feet slide backward and are buried in the sand. But you notice the beast is dazed.

You take advantage of this, jumping onto the bull's back and driving it downward, into the sand. The bull struggles and strains until its energy washes away. The animal collapses, exhausted, and it sleeps.

A crowd gathers in the sand. The people erupt in cheers, as you heft the bull across your shoulders. You carry it back along the sand until you reach the docks. There, you drop the Cretan Bull at Thelion's feet.

The sea captain eyes the beast, then shakes his head. "It will be a long voyage home with that creature tied up in our hold," he says.

Go to page 155.

8
A Gift from the Amazons

When the door to the palace opens, it is not King Eurystheus who appears. It is his assistant, Copreus.

"Our lord is seeking a gift for his daughter, the fair Admete," he says. "He wishes you to bring for her the Belt of Hippolyte."

"Hippolyte? Queen of the Amazons?" you ask.

Copreus nods.

The Amazons are a race of warrior women who live in a faraway land called Themiscrya. They are brave, strong, and fierce.

"Am I to steal the belt?" you ask.

"It is not my place to tell you how to complete your task. Do you take issue with this labor?" Copreus asks.

"No. I will be off at first light tomorrow."

Thelion also hears of your newest chore. When you arrive at the harbor, he and his men are preparing the ship with supplies.

You set sail the next morning. It is a long journey, but the seas are calm and the going is smooth.

After nearly a month, you reach the mouth of the river Thermodon. There, you see a harbor filled with wide wooden docks. There is no city to be found, though. Just a rocky shoreline, a clearing, and a dense forest that looks like a wall of trees.

A few ships are docked in the harbor, but there is plenty of space for Thelion and his men to tie up your ship. As they do, one of the men shouts, "Hercules, look over there!"

Three women approach the ship. They are tall and muscular, clothed in leather armor and carrying long spears. They are not angered by your presence, but they do not offer a warm welcome.

You climb down onto the dock, and then you kneel before them.

"Greetings," you say. "I am Hercules. I seek your queen, the beautiful Hippolyte."

One of the women steps forward, while the others suddenly aim the points of their spears at your throat. "No simple man comes to our shores and calls on our queen," the closest woman snaps.

"I am no simple man," you say. "I am Hercules, the son of Zeus."

At the mention of your father's name, the Amazons lower their weapons.

The first woman says, "Get back aboard your ship. Should the queen wish to speak with you, she'll come."

They walk back down the dock, and they disappear behind the trees.

Go to the next page.

Much time passes. Before you know it, the sun has lowered in the sky.

One of your shipmates, an older fellow with deep creases in his face, says, "They will not return."

"How do you know this?" you ask.

"I've heard stories of the Amazons—how deeply they hate men. There are many legends of how they burn ships from the sea and enslave the survivors."

"Nonsense," you say, though you begin to wonder if indeed this is a trap.

Soon, it will be dark. If the Amazons are planning an ambush, that is when it will happen. But you cannot leave without completing your task. Will you stay with the ship and pray the legends are untrue? Or will you go ashore in search of Queen Hippolyte? What will you choose to do?

To wait for the queen, go to page 136.

To search for the queen, go to page 84.

You cannot pass on this opportunity. Cerberus will not expect you to stand tall and face him head-on, so that's exactly what you do. You muster up every bit of strength within you. When the hound reaches you, you drive your fist into the jaw of Cerberus's middle head.

Crack!

The three-headed dog stands stunned for a moment, and then it falls, rolling into the stone wall beside the gates to the Underworld. The earth splits and the ground trembles.

Rocks begin to rain from above. A large boulder strikes one of the beast's heads. It hangs limp as the other heads whimper in pain. A shower of stones pours down on you, and you lift one arm above your head to shield yourself.

A boulder lands not two feet from you. You search for somewhere to hide. The bone gates slam shut; Hades will not allow you to enter.

Another stone, this one five times your size, hits the floor right in front of you. Startled, you step backward—straight into the River Styx.

As you try to lift your leg from the black water, a ghostly hand reaches up and grabs your ankle.

"Begone!" you shout, remembering Persephone's word from earlier.

It does not work. A second hand rises from the water and grabs your calf. Its touch is cold. Freezing cold.

The hands begin to pull, and you cannot fight them. They draw you into the river.

As if in quicksand, first one leg and then the other sinks below the water's surface. Soon, you are up to your waist. And there are many hands clawing at you. You give up the fight and allow yourself to be dragged under the black water of the River *Styx*—where your soul will rest for all eternity.

Go to page 83.

The giant is sleeping; you will never have a better opportunity to steal the cattle than right now.

Crouching low, you sneak past the house and down to the pasture. You quickly gather the cows and prepare to lead them back to Thelion's ship.

Suddenly, there is a growl behind you. You whirl around. Standing in the tall grass is a giant dog with two heads. It has black and white fur and powerful, wide paws.

The hound lets out three sharp, horrifying barks, and the snoring inside the house stops. You can hear—and even feel—the thuds as the giant lumbers to his feet.

"Orthus?" Geryon calls to his pet. He emerges from the home and looks around. He is one of the ugliest creatures you've ever seen. He has three bodies that are joined at the waist. His skin is gray and scaled.

When he sees you, Geryon throws back his heads and gives a mighty roar that bends the trees and shakes the earth at your feet.

As you attempt to flee, Orthus bounds to the right, its jaws snapping at you. Its teeth chomp down on your trusty club. They split the wood and nearly take off your hand. You swing your fist at the dog, but its tail strikes you in the chest and knocks you off your feet.

You land facedown in the dirt, gasping for breath.

Thundering footfalls approach. You roll onto your back to stare up at the blue sky. But instead, you gaze upon the three-bodied giant.

Geryon raises one foot high above you. You lift your weakened arms to shield your face. The giant's foot drops down, and you are squashed like a bug.

Go to page 83.

You're much faster than this beast; you're sure of it. You will not wait for it to make the first move. You run toward the animal before it can attack.

As you near the bull, you raise both hands. If you grab its horns, you can bring it down to the ground with ease. But the bull suddenly bucks to one side, and your fingers grab at nothing but air. You have misjudged the beast's quickness.

The powerful creature twists and swings its head in your direction. Pain shoots through your chest. You look down to see that one of the bull's coral horns has struck you.

Blackness fills your vision, as your life flows out of you. You are not yet immortal, and you never will be.

Go to page 83.

Dropping to one knee, you set the club in the sand and draw out your bow. A simple arrow will not stop the giant, so your aim must be precise. You notch an arrow into the bowstring and take a deep breath. With a soft *thwack*, you let the arrow fly.

Your aim is true. The arrow strikes the giant directly in one eye. Geryon roars and flails about, swinging his spears. One of the spears slices a tree in half; another is driven into the sand just a few feet from you.

Geryon drops to his knees, an action that shakes the very earth. The three-bodied giant blocks your path to the shore, but you cannot hesitate. You rush forward, weaving through the monster's legs. As you pass, he claws at you, but his massive fingers clutch only sand.

Diving into the cold sea, you swim to Thelion's ship. You're lucky to have survived your battle with the giant, and now you wish for a safe, quiet voyage home.

Go to page 117.

You have your doubts that the queen will return, but you decide that going ashore will anger Hippolyte. So you say, "We will wait. Thelion, prepare your men in case the Amazons attack. Let's hope, however, that we won't need to fight."

The men arm themselves with swords and shields. You do the same, keeping your eyes on the shoreline for any signs of movement.

Then, as dusk settles, you see several torches emerge from the trees. The women from earlier lead the way. Behind them is Queen Hippolyte. She is taller than the others, with raven-colored hair and a golden cloak about her shoulders. On her head is a crown, and around her wrists are large, golden bracelets.

As before, you kneel and introduce yourself.

"Stand," Queen Hippolyte says. "What is it you've come for, son of Zeus?"

You explain, "I am enslaved by King Eurystheus. He has sent me to retrieve the belt about your waist."

Beneath the queen's cloak, you spy a glimpse of the belt. It is armor made of pure gold.

Hippolyte throws back her head and laughs.

"And what makes you think I would part with my treasure?" she says

"Permit me, if I may, to tell you of my service to the king." You tell the queen stories of your adventures.

When you finish, the queen shakes her head in wonder. "I'm truly amazed," she says. "For telling such a fantastic tale, I will gladly give you the item you seek." She draws back the golden cloak and begins to remove the dazzling belt.

As she does, you notice a ruckus growing on the shoreline. More Amazons, these on horseback, join the queen's guards. They are fully armored, with shields and spears and swords. They shout angrily to one another.

The woman in the lead is hard to see in the moonlight, but she looks shockingly like Hera.

It cannot be, you think.

She cries out, "They have come to kidnap our queen! We must stop them!"

Hippolyte hears this and stops what she's doing. "Is that true?" she asks.

You quickly shake your head. "I only seek the belt."

"Attack!" shout the Amazons on the shore.

The men aboard Thelion's ship draw their weapons in fear. The queen sees this, and she quickly sheds her cloak and draws her sword.

"Our deal is off," she says.

You have no choice but to draw your own sword.

As the Amazons dismount and rush toward the ship, the queen strikes. She is fast; you are barely able to block her swing.

Metal clangs around you as Thelion's men and the Amazons engage in battle.

The ship's captain shouts, "Retreat!"

Men rush to the dock and untie the ship. Though it is dangerous to sail in shallow waters at night, you all must risk it.

You match Queen Hippolyte, blow for blow, your swords dancing. She is a strong fighter; it has been a long while since you had a challenge like this.

Finally, you see an opening and swing your sword down upon her. The blow glances off the queen's sword, knocking her to one knee. She is dazed, and her belt is exposed. With one quick move, it could be yours.

"Light the ship afire!"

The cry comes from behind you. Two Amazons with torches are climbing aboard the ship. If they are not stopped, they will set fire to the ship.

The belt is nearly yours; this could be your only chance to get it. But do you have enough time to take it? Or should you abandon your fight with Hippolyte to stop the torchbearers? What will you choose to do?

To grab the belt, go to page 142.

To stop the torchbearers, go to page 97.

You don't have many arrows left, so they must be saved for a sure shot. And with the dog rushing at you so fast, you fear that your aim would be poor. You draw the club from your belt, plant your feet, and wait for the slobbering canine.

When it is within ten yards of you, it crouches low and pounces into the air. You swing your club. There is a thunderous sound as the club connects, and the canine falls to the sand, unconscious.

Tree trunks split and the earth trembles as Geryon appears. He wears armor on his bodies and helmets on his heads. In three hands he holds huge spears. Each point is longer than your entire body. In his other three hands, the giant carries metal shields, each the size of a barn wall. He raises his spears and advances on you.

If you dipped your arrows in blood, go to page 116.

If not, go to page 135.

Charon told you to stay on the path, but Hades's throne room is within sight. And the ghosts have blocked the tunnel. You fear what they will do if they're able to catch you.

You dash off the path and toward the new tunnel, barely dodging the nearest lost souls as they reach out to grab you.

"Hades, it is I, Herc—"

Suddenly, you see nothing but a wall of rock. There is no throne room. No Hades. Nothing but . . .

"A dead end?"

The ghosts begin to drift closer, to swarm around you. You try to retreat but there is nowhere to run. Pale hands reach for you. They claw at your arms and legs. Their touch is cold, far colder than anything you've ever felt before. They seem to drain your life.

More and more of the lost souls surround you. You close your eyes, and soon they overtake you.

Go to page 83.

You can deal with the torchbearing Amazons in a moment. First, you must snatch the belt. This is too great an opportunity to pass up.

As you reach for the belt, Queen Hippolyte drives her elbow into your side, knocking the wind from you. Rising to her feet, she brings her sword up and slashes down at you. You block the blow with only a second to spare.

"Fire on deck!" Thelion's cry fills the night, and you turn to see that the Amazons have indeed lit the ship's sail on fire.

Soon, the whole ship is ablaze. You remain locked in battle with Queen Hippolyte, but you realize it doesn't matter. You've failed.

The wood beneath your feet cracks and splinters. Soot and ashes swirl about you. Amazons and sailors dive for the safety of the sea.

The ship's deck suddenly splits in two, and you feel the heat of the fire lick your skin. You fall toward the sea. Its cold water is the last sensation you ever feel.

Go to page 83.

You do not trust Atlas. It could all be a trick to get you to take over his burden. You would spend forever at the top of this mountain, holding the sky.

You shake your head. "I do not accept your offer. I will go after the apples myself."

"Very well," Atlas says. "You will find the garden at the north edge of the known world."

Atlas could easily be lying to you. If so, you'll never find the garden. But you'll have to take his word.

As you walk away, Atlas tells you, "Remember, the Hesperides are more dangerous than they seem."

You travel far to the north. The forests are thick there, lush with plant life. You scour the region for months in search of the garden.

At long last, you see it, and it's beautiful. At its center is the tree that bears golden apples. Its tall trunk is flecked with gold, and its branches are heavy with fruit.

Three beautiful women stand around the tree. Flowers decorate their hair. They are not the scary creatures Atlas made them out to be.

You approach the garden. When the Hesperides see you, they smile. One of them waves. They gather at the entrance of the garden.

"Welcome," the first woman says.

"How can we . . ." the second starts.

". . . help you?" the third woman finishes.

You are relieved. Surely, the women will let you bring back some of the apples.

"My name is Hercules," you tell them. "I was sent by your father, Atlas. I am to fetch some golden apples."

"Oh," says the first woman.

"I don't think . . ." starts the second.

". . . we can allow that," finishes the third.

You're confused. As you open your mouth to speak, the three women begin to sing. Their voices are perfect. Although you don't understand the words to their song, you find the tune quite soothing.

From near the tree, there is movement. At first, you think the tree is alive. Then you notice a creature. It is a dragon: a beast with nearly a hundred heads and a long tail speckled with gold. Their song has summoned this monster.

"You see," says the first woman.

"Our friend, Ladon . . ." starts the second.

". . . does not like when someone takes our apples," finishes the third.

The dragon towers over you. You draw your weapon but are afraid it will do no good. Not this time.

Atlas spoke the truth: the Hesperides are far more dangerous than you expected.

One of the dragon's heads strikes in front of you. A second head attacks from behind. Its strong jaws clamp around your middle and pull you off the ground.

Ladon tosses you into the air, and for a second you realize that you are about to become a dragon's meal. Then the beast swallows you whole.

Go to page 83.

Your quiver is half full of arrows, and it's safer to stop the beast before his snapping jaws get too close. You drop to a knee and draw out your bow.

You notch the first arrow and let it fly. It slices in between the dog's heads, missing its target. A second shot strikes the dirt at its feet.

As you release a third arrow, Geryon appears. He has donned armor and helmets. In three hands he holds massive spears. Each point is longer than your entire body. In his other three hands, the giant carries metal shields, each the size of a barn wall.

His appearance has distracted you, and your shot goes wide. You have one arrow left.

The slobbering dog is yards away. You take a breath to steady yourself, notch the arrow, and let it fly. It does not hit the beast directly but glances off one of the dog's legs. The canine stumbles and hits the dirt hard.

"Orthus!" Geryon's cry fills the air. He raises his spears and advances on you.

You prepare your club to defend yourself. However, Geryon is fast. Before you can attack, he swings one of the spears and hits you directly in the chest.

You soar through the air and land in the shallow water of the sea. You stagger to your feet, preparing to defend yourself against the giant. But Geryon has seen Thelion's ship sailing away with his cattle.

He heaves one of his spears toward it. It hits the ship's hull and splinters the wooden vessel. You hear men on the deck panic as water begins to fill the ship. Within moments, the ship has sunk below the surface of the sea.

You stand, grip your wooden club with both hands, and face Geryon. You no longer care about the outcome of this fight, though. You've failed. Now the gods will never grant you immortality. Geryon roars, lifts his two remaining spears, and attacks.

Go to page 83.

You nod. "I'm going to trust you, Atlas," you say. "I will take your burden, as long as you bring back a handful of golden apples from your daughters."

"I will," he responds.

You stand beside the huge man. Atlas kneels. You raise your arms to receive the burden of the heavens. At first, when Atlas places the sun and sky upon your shoulders, it does not seem so heavy. Quite light, in fact. You say as much to Atlas.

"It's deceiving," he says. With the burden lifted off him, he seems a different man. "The longer you hold them, the heavier they grow."

"Then be quick," you say.

Atlas nods. "I will." He bounds down the mountain.

As days pass, the load bears down on you. Your legs begin to burn as if they were on fire. Your shoulders ache. You cannot imagine living an eternity like this.

Just as you begin to believe that Atlas has tricked you into taking his place for good, he returns. He carries a sack over his shoulder. When he reaches you, Atlas drops the sack. Inside, you see the flash of golden fruit.

He has done it; Atlas has completed the task.

You prepare to hand the heavens back to him. "I cannot wait to see the look upon King Eurystheus's face when I hand the apples to him."

Atlas thinks for a moment, then says, "You know, neither can I."

"What do you mean?" But you know what he means.

"I will finish this labor for you, Hercules," Atlas explains. "I will go to Mycenae and give him the apples myself. It feels so wonderful to be free from the weight of the sky. You do not mind holding the heavens a bit longer, do you?"

Of course, you do. This was never part of your deal.

Atlas scoops up the sack. "Goodbye, Hercules."

You must think quickly. If you let Atlas out of your sight, you'll be forced to hold the heavens for eternity.

"Atlas, wait!" The trickster stops and turns back to you. "Return quickly from Mycenae, will you?"

Atlas smiles. "I will."

"Oh," you add, "I must also move the lion pelt upon my shoulders, to use as a cushion. Do you mind taking my place for a moment while I do this?"

Atlas lays the sack of apples atop a rock. "Not at all," he says.

He kneels beside you and takes the burden back onto his shoulders. You breathe deeply. It feels wonderful to be free again.

You dash over to the sack of fruit and pluck it off the rock. "Many thanks," you say.

Understanding flashes in Atlas's eyes, and his face twists in rage. "You!" He lifts his head and screams.

Dark clouds swirl in the sky. Lightning flashes within them. You hear Atlas shouting your name until well after he is out of sight.

11
Guardians of the Underworld

King Eurystheus is not pleased to see you. He hurls one of the golden apples at the wall. The fruit splatters against the marble. The remainder of the sack lies at the foot of his throne.

"Shall I take them back?" you ask with a smile.

The king is not amused. He is silent for a long while, and it almost looks as if he's waiting for advice from an unseen partner.

"What does Hera say, cousin?"

Eurystheus is startled by your question. His eyes darken, and he says, "I have one labor left for you. Then your time as my servant is done. You shall be free to seek out the gods and request your place among them."

Soon, everything you've worked for these past ten years will be yours. "And what is this final task?" you ask eagerly.

"Bring me Cerberus."

Cerberus is a terrible beast: the Underworld's guard dog. It stands nearly twenty feet tall, with three heads and a serpent's tail.

Hades, brother of Zeus and Poseidon, rules the Underworld. Upon mortal death, all souls are sent to the Underworld to be judged for eternity. It is Hades's job to welcome them. It is Cerberus's job to protect them.

As far as labors go, King Eurystheus has certainly kept the most difficult and dangerous for last. No mortal has ever returned from the Underworld. You only hope that your standing as Hades's nephew will help you be the first to come back.

"Very well," you say, turning and leaving at once.

There is a stretch of land in the far south, in a place called Taenarum. An area of rock stands at the end of the earth, surrounded by sea. Within these stones is a crack in the earth that leads down into blackness. Down to the Underworld.

You walk within this rocky tomb. It is pitch black, so you must use one hand to guide you. In the other is your wooden club. Your hand slides along the damp stone as you descend. From time to time, a cobweb strings across your path, and you blindly swat it away.

For hours you stumble along in darkness. And then you see a tiny flicker of light in the distance. You try not to hurry to it, for fear that you will trip and hurt yourself. The flicker grows larger, until you can make out what it is: a fire.

You reach the bottom of the cave, where the flame rests within a metal bowl. The fire shines light on your surroundings. To your left, there is another dark cave. You've heard tales that, within this cave, there may be a secret passage that could lead you to Hades.

To your right is a wide, black river that smells of sulfur. Beside the river stands a man. He is skinny and stooped, with a long, wispy beard, pointed ears, and hollow eyes. Behind him on the riverbank is a small wooden boat.

He waves one withered hand at you. "Come," he croaks. "I am Charon. Climb aboard my boat. I can shepherd you across the River Styx."

If the man before you is telling the truth, he will lead you to Hades. If not, he could trap your soul in the Underworld for eternity. There is also the other cave, the one to your left. Maybe you'll find the correct path to your uncle's throne that way. Should you accept Charon's offer, or will you explore the other cave? What will you choose to do?

To travel with Charon, go to page 122.

To explore the cave, go to page 104.

Your eighth labor is a much simpler matter. You travel to the city of Thrace, far to the north of Mycenae. There, the cruel King Diomedes has driven his horses mad and has turned them into man-eating beasts.

With your strength and cunning, you free the horses. You show them kindness and compassion, and you are eventually able to tame the creatures. When they're back to full health, you return with them to your cousin.

"King Eurystheus!" you exclaim. "Come and see these majestic animals!"

The four horses are nearly identical: tall and lean, with sleek black coats and silken manes.

"They are quite tame now," you continue. "There is nothing to fear." You run one hand over the muzzle of the nearest horse.

Go to page 126.

Epilogue:
Facing Your Fear

Your eyes flutter open. You're back in the library, huddled in the corner. Yet now there is nothing in your hands. The shelf beside you is empty. Where have the books gone? Was everything just a dream?

Mrs. Englehopper, the school librarian, pushes a cart of books past your hiding place. When she sees you, she stops. "Are you all right?" she asks.

It's a good question. Before you found that book, you probably would've answered, "No." Now, though, you know how to handle Tyler Hammond.

"I'm okay," you tell her.

"If you need to catch a bus, I suggest you hurry."

With a glance at the empty shelf where you found the Hercules book, you stand and exit the library.

Like Cerberus guarding the gates of the Underworld, Tyler Hammond stands before the line of school buses. But you are no longer afraid of him. You walk down the steps. Students notice you and stop to watch. They whisper to one another.

Tyler sees you coming and his face wrinkles into a scowl. "About time you got here," he says.

He cracks his knuckles, trying to scare you. It doesn't work. You've learned from your adventure that bravery means different things at different times.

You walk right up to him. He sizes you up, like he's looking for the perfect place to punch you.

You smile. "Hey, Tyler," you say cheerfully.

He looks surprised, then confused. You're supposed to be afraid of him, not friendly and confident.

Tyler stammers, "Um . . . hey."

"Sorry again about your shirt."

"Th—that's okay. Um, don't let it happen again."

You nod. "See you tomorrow." You smile again and walk past him.

You climb the steps of your bus, squeeze down the narrow aisle, and find a spot to sit. The kids around you pretend they weren't watching.

The bus rumbles and coughs. Then it pulls away from the curb, and you are on your way home.

Go to the next page.

The End

You have survived
the Twelve Labors
of Hercules!

CAN YOU SURVIVE?

Test your survival skills with a free
short story at **www.Lake7Creative.com**,
and pick up these Choose Your Path books:

- *Bram Stoker's Dracula*
- *Greek Mythology's Adventures of Perseus*
- *Howard Pyle's Merry Adventures of Robin Hood*
- *Jack London's Call of the Wild*
- *Jules Verne's 20,000 Leagues Under the Sea*
- *Robert Louis Stevenson's Treasure Island*
- *Sir Arthur Doyle's Adventures of Sherlock Holmes*

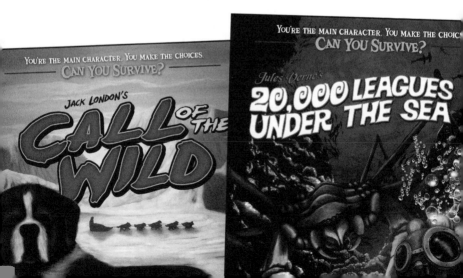

About Myths

Myths started out as oral tellings of popular stories. Ancient storytellers would go from village to village telling stories to people. These stories, or myths as we now call them, would then be passed from person to person and be retold over and over again.

During the retellings, storytellers often changed things. They'd make the monsters more horrifying. The heroes more brave. The fights more dramatic. They did this to keep their audiences entertained. The more excited people were to hear the stories, the more popular the storytellers became.

That's why there are so many different versions of some myths. Throughout the years, storytellers created their own versions. Sometimes, the names of people and places changed. Even in this adaptation, some details have changed. The book incorporates parts from many variations of Hercules's adventures.

All the unique versions of ancient myths are what make reading them interesting. Each storyteller has his or her own interpretation of the story.

About the Author

When Brandon Terrell was a boy, he was tall and skinny and looked nothing like Hercules. But he was a big fan of comic books (he still is!) and superheroes. Hercules was always at the top of that list. Right next to Spider-Man, of course.

Nowadays, Brandon doesn't face serpents with a hundred heads or have the proportionate strength of a spider. He does, however, enjoy writing stories about amazing heroes and incredible adventures. He is the author of numerous books, including chapter books, picture books, and graphic novels. Brandon lives in Saint Paul, Minnesota, with his wife Jennifer and their two children.